If I Were You

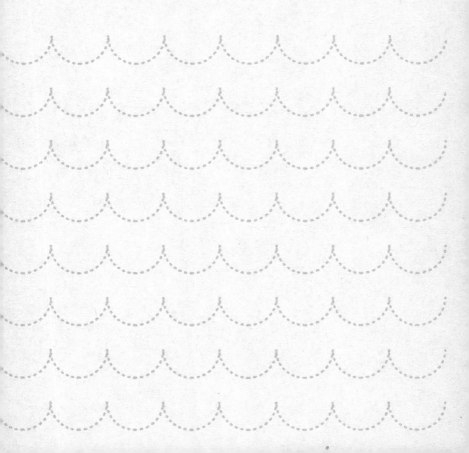

IF I WERE YOU

LESLIE MARGOLIS

SQUARE FISH

FARRAR STRAUS GIROUX • NEW YORK

SQUARE FISH

An Imprint of Macmillan
175 Fifth Avenue
New York, NY 10010
mackids.com

Our books may be purchased in bulk for promotional, educational, or business
use. Please contact your local bookseller or the Macmillan Corporate and
Premium Sales Department at (800) 221-7945 ext. 5442 or by e-mail
at MacmillanSpecialMarkets@macmillan.com.

Library of Congress Cataloging-in-Publication Data
Margolis, Leslie.
    If I were you / Leslie Margolis.
        pages cm
    Summary: Twelve-year-old best friends Katie and Melody have had a terrible
summer, ending with a fight over a boy, but when Katie's wish to begin the
summer over as Melody comes true, each girl learns important lessons about the
other and herself.
    ISBN 978-1-250-07974-9 (paperback)   ISBN 978-0-374-30069-2 (ebook)
    [1. Best friends—Fiction.   2. Friendship—Fiction.   3. Identity—Fiction.
4. Wishes—Fiction.   5. Magic—Fiction.]   I. Title.

PZ7.M33568lf 2015
[Fic]—dc23

                                                                2014041190

Originally published in the United States by Farrar Straus Giroux
First Square Fish Edition: 2016
Square Fish logo designed by Filomena Tuosto

10   9   8   7   6   5   4   3   2

LEXILE: 690L

For Lucy and Leo

If I WERE YOU

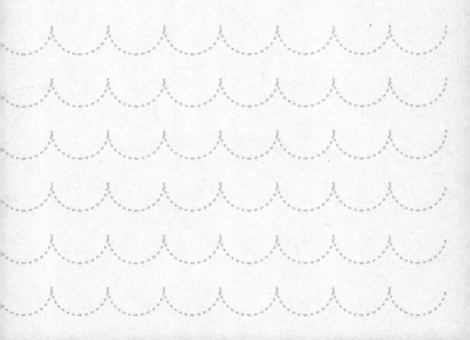

KATIE

Betrayed on the Beach Bus

Summer was a disaster. I'm talking epic failure. And it's all Melody's fault. Which is ironic because she's supposed to be my best friend and this was supposed to be the best summer of our lives.

We both turned twelve in June, which meant we were finally old enough to take the bus to Crescent Moon Bay on our own. Crescent Moon Bay, in case you didn't know, is the most spectacular beach in Malibu.

Melody and I had a gazillion plans, none of which involved her stealing my future boyfriend or me getting stuck taking my four-year-old stepbrothers to the beach, solo. Yet here we are. It's the last day of summer and Kevin's got his arm around Melody. And me? I'm holding hands with Ryan and Reese, the three of us sticky and smelling like chunky peanut butter and blueberry jam.

The beach bus leaves every hour, so it's simply bad luck that we happen to be on the same one. It's even worse luck that Melody and Kevin got on first and chose the third row, so the boys and I have no choice but to walk past them.

At least they're completely wrapped up in each other. That means they might not notice me, although I am hard to miss. I am an albatross, except not as graceful, weighed down not only by my stepbrothers but also by the largest tote bag in the universe. I'm carrying lunches, towels, sunscreen, and too many toys: soccer balls, baseballs, buckets and shovels, big plastic trucks, and a gigantic stuffed turtle in sunglasses that the boys insisted they could not survive without.

We've only just gotten on and Ryan is already asking if we're almost there.

"The bus isn't even moving yet," I whisper.

"When's it going to go?" asks Reese.

"Once everyone is sitting down." We're about to pass Melody and Kevin. I'm sure they can hear us and I wish Reese would keep his voice down.

"I have a rock in my shoe," Ryan announces.

"The sunglasses are falling off Turtle," Reese says, even louder.

It's like they're trying to humiliate me.

"Can we please keep moving?" I hurry them forward, almost in tears at the injustice of everything. Melody is the one who promised to take Ryan and Reese to the beach in the first place. Of course, that was before I spied her and Kevin kissing in her hot tub last Saturday night.

But I don't want to dwell on that, because as furious and as mortified as I am, deep down I can't help but wish that she were hanging out with us. Things are always easier when Melody is around. She has this sweet and gentle way about her. Plus, Ryan and Reese actually listen to her. My mom says it's because she's not their stepsister and they don't get to see her as often. But I know the truth. My stepbrothers listen to Melody because even though they are only four, they are still boys and all boys like Melody better.

The two of us represent the universal rule of opposites. Melody is a boy magnet. I'm more like boy repellent.

We are almost past the ecstatic couple, practically in the clear, when Ryan spots Melody and shouts her name at the top of his lungs. *"Melo!"*

Melo is our nickname for Melody. It stands for both *mellow* because she is by nature, and also *marshmallow* because she loves them so much. Whenever we make s'mores in her fire pit, she roasts herself at least three extra marshmallows.

Kevin and Melody look over at us, surprised expressions on their faces.

Ryan drops my hand and climbs onto their seat even though there's hardly any room. Melody inches closer to Kevin to make space, so now their legs are actually touching.

"Hi, guys," says Melody, brightening at the sight of my stepbrothers. She tousles Ryan's hair, smiles at Reese, and does not raise her gaze to acknowledge me.

Kevin ignores me, too, and it hurts. "Hey, little dudes," he says sweetly, as he leans over Melody and offers up his hand. "Who wants to give me five?"

Ryan and Reese fight over who gets to slap Kevin's hand first.

Meanwhile, I sniff back tears, grateful that my eyes are hidden behind gigantic sunglasses, the frames of which are heart shaped and red with sparkles. Yes, my shades are hideous and out of style by several decades but I am wearing them ironically. That's what I intended, anyway. At the moment I have the feeling that they simply look ridiculous. At least they're hiding my watery eyes. I stand up straighter, shove the stuffed turtle farther into my bag, and try to maintain some dignity.

"Can we sit with you, Melody?" Reese asks in his

sweetest, most pleading little voice. There's clearly no room, and when he tries to join them, Ryan shoves him off the seat, wanting Melody all to himself.

My former best friend smiles and tells him gently, "I wish there was more room. I'll sit with you next time. Okay?"

"Promise?" asks Reese.

"I promise," Melody says solemnly, holding up her right hand like the dutiful Girl Scout she used to be.

"Come on, let's go," I say, taking Ryan's elbow and pulling him off their seat.

He looks up at me and asks, "Are you crying?"

"Be quiet!" I hiss, pushing both boys down the aisle. My tremendous bag is knocking into strangers left and right—I hear some grunts, a couple of ouches— but I don't even look back or apologize, I'm in such a hurry.

"I want to sit near Melo," Ryan whines.

"We can't!" I say, feeling like the meanest big sister in the world.

The three of us squish into a seat twelve rows back. We are out of earshot of Kevin and Melody but close enough for me to admire Kevin's perfect head.

He's wearing a faded red baseball cap. He is golden in every sense of the word—his tan, his shaggy hair, his long, lean limbs, and his whole entire aura. I am swooning and telling myself to stop, but this only makes me swoon harder. Gah!

At least he and Melody aren't all over each other anymore. She's now reading a book. Kevin is staring straight ahead, probably doing something cool like meditating or visualizing himself on a surfboard or planning some romantic date with Melo or silently reciting obscure poetry. Maybe he's doing all of this simultaneously.

I don't know what her problem is. If I were Melody I would not be reading some boring book. I would be paying attention to the perfect specimen of a guy right next to me.

When I notice her yawn I almost lose it. This is so unfair I want to scream! Melody and I agreed that Kevin was mine. We worked it out months ago because Melody does not like Kevin as much as I do. She can't! And even if she did, I saw him first. Plus, how much luck and happiness does one girl deserve? Melody already has everything: perfect parents who are still married and actually get along and a ginormous house with her own hot tub and pool with a slide.

Oh, and let's not forget her looks. Melody is gorgeous. She's got curly blond hair that's silky smooth, with no hint of frizz. Her eyes are blue green like the Caribbean Sea, not that I have ever been to the Caribbean to know this. My knowledge comes from Ryan and Reese's jumbo box of crayons.

Melody knows the Caribbean because she goes on vacation with her grandmother there every single year. She's been everywhere: Turks and Caicos, Saint John's, Saint Thomas, Saint Bart's, and Barbados.

Wait. Is Barbados a part of the Caribbean? I suspect not, but I don't know for sure. Of course, it doesn't matter if I know or not. It's not like I'll ever get there.

The only place I travel to is Seattle because that's where my dad moved after my parents got divorced four years ago.

Let me tell you about Seattle: the mountains are green and spectacular looking, but it's impossible to enjoy them because it's always cold and gloomy and raining. Also, my dad is married to a taxidermist. So, yeah, my stepmom stuffs dead animals—for a living. She takes her work home with her, too. Their house is filled with all sorts of creatures, from tiny white mice to tremendous moose, and everything in between.

And did I mention I'm a vegetarian?

I'm a vegetarian, so being surrounded by dead animals—most of them hunted for sport and then stuffed for bragging rights—does not exactly sit well with me. That's why I don't visit very often. Only on the court-mandated every other Christmas, Thanksgiving, and Spring Break.

I spend most of my time in Braymar in a tiny, loud, supercrowded house with my mom and her new husband,

Jeff, and his kids, Ryan and Reese. The three of them moved in with us last year.

Jeff is a nice guy and I love his kids, too. It's the story of Jeff and my mom that gets to me. They were each other's first crushes and went out together for all of sixth grade until Jeff and his family moved to England. That means their love for each other at eleven was so pure and true that it lasted for years, through the trials and tribulations of life and moves to different continents, and marriage and kids with other people, until they finally got their happy ending.

That's what everyone always says. People love their story. And it's fine and wonderful and romantic for them, but it sure puts a gazillion tons of pressure on me. Because guess what? I am already twelve and I've never even had a boyfriend. Ever.

I've had plenty of crushes but as far as I know, none of those crushes have been returned. It's completely one-sided. I'm one hundred percent uncrushable. I promised myself that would change this summer. Things were supposed to come together for me after I graduated from sixth grade back in June. Summer stretched before me and I was finally ready to live life like a regular kid— break curfew, sneak out of the house, go to raging parties, and meet cute boys. Except none of that actually happened and middle school starts tomorrow. I failed. Big time. And now it's too late.

I will never have a sixth-grade boyfriend to break up with and then reunite with years later. I'll probably spend all of middle school alone. I won't even bother going to the dances. Why even show up when I'll have to stand around by myself? No one will ask me to dance, except maybe one of the chaperones out of pity. I'll become known as the loner sad sack and my rotten reputation will carry on into high school.

I will not go to homecoming.

I will not go to prom.

I will grow old and shriveled solo—bitter about my youth.

I might as well give up now and tell my mom I want to be homeschooled. Not that my mother even has time to homeschool me. She's too busy with work and with helping the twins adjust to our "blended family." But why am I complaining about that? It's not like I even want to spend more time with my mom at the moment.

I am so distraught I am not making sense, but at least we're almost at the beach. I've taken this route a million times and I know every turn on this winding, canyon road.

When Melody and I were in second grade, our moms took us to Crescent Moon Bay nearly every day of the summer. Back then, life was good and simple and fun. Melody and I were besties and we cared more about boogie boarding than boys.

The two of us always played the wishing game when we got to the Crescent Moon Tunnel, which marks the halfway point between our town and the beach. The tunnel is long and dark and dramatic, carved out of a gigantic mountain in the middle of the road. As soon as you clear it, you can see the ocean.

Transitioning from sleepy suburban town to spectacular Malibu beach within less than a minute is magical enough for me, but Melody always swore our wishes would come true if we followed the rules. "Hold your breath and keep your eyes shut tight and wish with all of your might," she'd remind me.

Back then I believed her and tried every single time.

That first summer, I kept wishing my parents would stop screaming at each other. Instead they got divorced. The second summer I wished for a pony for Christmas. When December rolled around, I got knitting lessons. Yes, knitting lessons. My mom thought they'd be a fun bonding experience for the two of us. She even phrased it like that: *We'll learn together and it'll be a fun bonding experience.* As if she were reading some self-help book on how to relate to your preteen daughter, one that was written a hundred years ago.

Long story short: the only thing we bonded over was how truly terrible the knitting lessons were.

I stopped making wishes after that, but today I close

my eyes. This is Labor Day, the last official day of summer. Tomorrow, I start seventh grade. Middle school! This is probably the last time I'll ever take the beach bus, and what have I got to lose?

I have no boyfriend and no best friend and no prospects for either.

I am squished between my stepbrothers.

Ryan is picking his nose but I don't have the energy to fight him on it. Reese is kicking the seat of the lady in front of us and I can tell that she is about to turn around and yell and then I'll have to deal with that, too. But at the moment, I am free.

I'm still wearing my sunglasses, so no one will ever guess what I'm doing. Plus, I know what I want. It comes to me fast, as if the idea were hardwired into my brain. And who am I kidding—it so totally is. My heart's desire is sad and silly, but painfully true.

I wish I could start this summer over, as Melody. I mumble the words under my breath because wishes only work if you say them out loud.

I hear Ryan ask "What?" and I see, out of the corner of my eye, that Reese is staring up at me with curiosity.

I ignore the boys, take a gulp of air, and hold my breath.

The bus races forward.

Even with my eyes squeezed tight I can tell we're in

the tunnel because everything is cool and dark. I feel the hairs on my arms stand up. Goose bumps form on my flesh and I shiver. I shut my eyes tighter and I wish with every fiber of my being that I were Melody.

Suddenly, strangely, I feel a strong tingling sensation, like I have pins and needles in my whole entire body. Then something shifts inside of me. At first, I think it's my soul. But that can't be. Souls do not shift and anyway, mine has been crushed.

Maybe I'm about to lose that egg-and-cheese sand-wich I wolfed down before we got to the bus. I've never been carsick before, but it would be just my luck and totally fitting for me to barf on the beach bus in front of Kevin.

True, we are sitting behind Kevin, but surely the smell would waft up. He'd probably turn around before I had a chance to wipe my face and—ugh—I can picture his look of horror.

Except then the shifting tingling sensation fades into oblivion. Now everything is back to normal, my stomach included.

The sun shines in through the windows, warming my limbs. We are out of the tunnel and I feel fine.

I open my eyes and see blue. This calms me. Life is pretty sucky—yes, Melody may have betrayed me and I officially have no chance with Kevin—but I'll always have

Crescent Moon Bay. I can already hear the waves crashing on the beach, smell the salty fresh air.

Then I realize something strange. I'm no longer sitting in the back of the bus. I'm more toward the middle. Also? Ryan and Reese have disappeared. Where'd they go? Did I lose my stepbrothers? If I lost my stepbrothers, I'll be so busted.

I look but don't see them anywhere. I'm not alone, though. Someone else is next to me, and she's about my size.

I squint and then gasp because I'm staring in the mirror. Except that's impossible. There is no mirror on this seat.

Still, I am looking at a replica of myself and it's not two-dimensional. I am looking at myself in the flesh because I am out of my own body.

"What's going on?" I ask myself. I mean the "me" who looks like me—the me, as in Katie, with the same long dark hair and green eyes and pale, freckly thighs sticking out of my cutoff shorts. The same shorts that I wore on the first day of summer and lost that very same day. My favorite shorts that I figured I'd never see again.

Now they turn up? Cool!

Except wait. How could I be wearing them at this moment, when they're not what I put on this morning?

And how could I not be myself?

Unless . . .

No, wishes don't come true. Especially not mine.

Yet this whole situation seems eerily similar to my real first day of summer.

"Katie, is that you?" the girl who looks like me asks. Her voice sounds exactly like my voice. The voice is mine and it's actually coming out of a mouth that is mine except it's not because I am not myself. I am no longer Katie.

I run my hands through my long and wild blond curls. I look down at the white cotton cardigan draped over the pink-and-white polka-dot sundress that flounces at the bottom. It's the outfit Melody wore on the first day of summer, the dress that only she can pull off.

And that's when I realize this insanely crazy impossible thing: my wish came true.

I am starting the summer over.

We are back to day one.

Except this time I'm Melody.

MELODY

Freckled Perfection

I'm Katie! I'm Katie! I'm Katie!

As we get off the bus and head toward the beach I have to keep myself from skipping. I feel as if I'm walking on gigantic, fluffy pink clouds of awesomeness. I cannot remember feeling so elated. Ever. Like in my whole entire life. Stunned, too, because this is actually happening.

I've envied Katie's life for years, wanted to be her for almost as long, and now here I am with skinny, freckled, pale arms and stick-straight hair and big green eyes that take everything in. I look like a dorky little kid in my red sparkly glasses and cutoff jeans shorts but that's okay. Better than okay, actually: it's perfect. I've dreamed of being a dorky little kid all summer. What could be more fun?

When Katie and I were younger we spent whole after-noons chalk drawing on the sidewalk and making mud pies and digging holes and skipping rope. Back then our moms drove us to the beach, where we chased waves for hours, wading through knee-deep water, scrawny chests puffed brave in the face of danger. At the first hint of the crash, we'd run back to our moms, screaming our heads off, collapsing into fits of giggles.

We built elaborate sand castle villages with moats and seaweed bridges and pebbled walkways. We raced up and down sand dunes and goofed off until our tummies ached from hunger. Then we crammed warm PB&Js into our mouths, laughing because even though the peanut butter was creamy, our sandwiches still somehow packed a crunch. We had the life, wiping our mouths with the backs of our tan, sticky hands, our shoulders freckling as the sun beamed down. Seagulls circled over our heads, eyeing our food.

More than once, those pesky birds—flying rats, Katie called them—made off with the better parts of our lunches and we cried real tears, heartbroken because sto-len potato chips and Oreos were our biggest problems in life back then.

We didn't care about boyfriends. We didn't care about boys, period.

These days my mom would rather be stabbed in the

eye than pack me any kind of food that does not come directly from an organic garden. Katie and I are too old for sand castles and splashing in the surf. Now, we bask in the sun and go for walks and talk, but summer continues to be magical and delicious. I wish for the season to start over every year in the wishing tunnel, holding my breath and crossing my fingers and my toes and squeezing my eyes shut so tight I see bursts of blue and red behind my eyelids, but to no avail.

Except for this year.

This year my wish was a little bit different.

This year I yearned with every inch of my body to start the summer over as Katie. And she must've wished for the exact same thing at the exact same time because it totally worked.

We've switched places!

"How awesome is this?" I ask Katie—the real Katie, who is currently occupying my body.

We're off the bus and in the parking lot and I'm so excited I'm jumping up and down. In Katie's body I feel lighter on my feet and freer, too. I can bounce around without worrying about random leering guys.

Katie is completely still and silent. She stares down at herself and then at me.

I pull her away from the crowd filing off the bus. "Katie?" I whisper. "It's you in there, right?"

"I'm Melody," she says as if in a trance.

"Yup," I say, grinning like mad. "You look like me and you even sound like me. But you've got your own brain. Isn't it awesome? I told you the wishing tunnel would work if we wanted something badly enough."

Katie shakes her head, stubborn as always. "That's impossible. People don't switch bodies in real life. This has got to be a dream. I must've fallen asleep on the ride to the beach. I just hope I'm not snoring or drooling. Or what if I'm snoring *and* drooling?"

I can't help but laugh at this. For all of Katie's faults, she's often hilarious. "You think you'd be this neurotic in a dream?" I ask.

She doesn't answer. She's not even paying attention to me. Instead, she's pacing across the parking lot, talking to herself like a crazy person.

"If Ryan and Reese witness that, they'll never let me live it down. And what if Kevin sees? How much mortification can one girl take?" She throws up her hands.

"Will you stop worrying," I say. "This is great news. We got exactly what we wanted and we can totally pull this off."

She ignores me. "Except, wait. I'm an extremely light sleeper. Always have been. If I drooled on myself I'd totally wake up. Same goes for snoring—I'd hear myself loud and clear."

"See," I say, grabbing her hand, so she'll finally pay attention, "this is no dream. Let's go!"

I pull her toward the beach. Crescent Moon Bay is stunning as always. I kick off my sandals and sink my feet into the warm sand. I wiggle my toes. Katie's toes. They're painted red with sparkles. We gave each other pedicures the night before. Katie loves everything red and sparkly—that's what she always goes for. But I like to mix things up. Last night I chose pink with white polka dots to match my dress. Then, on my big toenails, I made white hearts outlined in turquoise. They look pretty awesome, if I do say so myself.

But who cares about nail polish when we're finally in Malibu. The water is so blue, so endless and wild it makes my breath catch in my throat. The crashing waves are music to my ears, my favorite sound. I breathe in deeply. The air smells like summer and possibility, that magical combination of saltwater and coconut sunscreen, hot dogs and French fry grease.

"It feels so real," Katie marvels, holding her free hand in front of her face.

"That's because it is real," I reply, wondering how many times I'm going to have to tell her.

"Oh wow. Look at Kevin," Katie says, squeezing my hand.

As Kevin walks by with his green backpack slung over

his shoulder and his surfboard tucked under one arm, I feel a little queasy. Kevin is the last person I want to see right now. He's the reason that Katie and I aren't talking. Weren't talking, I mean.

Now that it's the beginning of summer, I'm confused.

We're talking now, obviously, but in our old reality, back at the end of summer? Well, that's a long and complicated story. And it's Kevin's fault. Kind of, in the sense that if he didn't exist then we wouldn't be having this problem. Okay, I guess I need to take some of the blame, since I did sneak around a bit behind Katie's back, but I never meant to hurt her. I kept him a secret because I didn't want her to get upset. But obviously my plan backfired.

"Are you still mad at me?" I ask.

My best friend looks at me. It's weird staring at her, staring into my own eyes. It's not quite my mirror image because she's a real flesh-and-blood person I could reach out and poke in the stomach, not that I would.

"I'm not going to waste this totally amazing dream being mad at you," she says.

I bite my bottom lip, happy we're not fighting but still nervous. "What if this isn't a dream?" I ask.

"It's day one of summer," she says with a shrug. "We're starting over. Today is the first time we see Kevin but neither of us actually knows the guy, right?"

I nod and say, "Um, right."

Except as soon as the words leave my mouth I regret them. The problem? I lied again. Katie thinks we both met Kevin for the first time on the Fourth of July. But actually I met Kevin way sooner, over Christmas vacation when he was visiting his dad. Except I kept it a secret. And that's what got me into this mess in the first place: Kevin and lying and lying about Kevin.

It started out innocently, I swear. I thought I was telling a small fib, but then it grew. And grew. And grew.

It's just like that web of lies my dad used to warn me about. You tell one lie and then you have to tell another lie to make that first lie plausible. And then you have to tell another one to cover for yourself, and then another and another and soon your lies are piling up on top of one another and you're in a big sticky mess, caught like a fly.

I am a fly in that web. Stuck. And now we're back in time. And I got myself stuck all over again.

I wasn't expecting this now that I'm Katie. Life should be easier, less complicated. That's the problem with boys. They complicate things.

Like with Kevin. As soon as Katie laid eyes on him she told me she was in love, that she was going to go out with him. And we agreed that she could have him because she called dibs first, except we didn't actually agree. Katie simply decided for the two of us.

That's how it's always been with me and Katie. She makes the rules and I follow along. We've operated like that for the past ten years. That's how long we've been besties. Since before we could even speak in complete sentences. But things have been different lately. I'm different—or at least I want to be. We're going into middle school and I don't want to spend all of seventh grade following Katie around. I actually don't even want to spend another day following her around.

Of course, even though I made that decision, I never actually got around to telling her. Maybe that's part of the problem.

K Surprise!

I look like Melody and I feel kind of like Melody, too. Even though body swapping does not happen in real life, I've already wasted too much time freaking out over the switch. I may as well enjoy this dream.

"Let's find a spot near the water," I say, picking up Melody's pristine white tote bag and slinging it over my shoulder. The towel inside is rolled neatly. It's pink-and-turquoise striped, plush, and expensive-looking. Nicer than my old towel, but I am not surprised. Of course Melody's got the nicest, prettiest towel in Malibu. Her tote bag, too, is brand-new. Inside are four pouches in different, coordinating colors—light pink, dark rose, baby blue, and lavender. I've never seen them before and Melo probably hadn't, either.

Melody's mom is a big shopper. Practically every sales-person in town knows her by name. Plus, boxes from Bar-neys and Bloomingdale's and stores I've never even heard of appear on her doorstep daily. Melody has so much new stuff I can't keep track of everything. She can't either sometimes.

I take out the light pink pouch and unzip it. Inside I find carrots, celery, and jicama sticks. Nice! Melody's mom packed me a snack. Packed Melody a snack, I mean. And I'm Melody. This was so superthoughtful of her, even though, rummaging around in the bag, I can tell that she forgot the dip.

I can't complain, though, because my actual real-life mom never has time for stuff like that. She's a public de-fender who's superbusy with work and with the process of officially adopting Ryan and Reese. They don't have another mom, for reasons too sad for me to get into right now. And I'm proud of my mom for stepping up, but I'm also acutely aware of the fact that without me, she and Jeff and the twins would be the perfect nuclear family. They look like they belong together, too. The twins al-ready call her Mom and the three of them have reddish-blond hair and big blue eyes.

And me? When I'm *not* dreaming about being Melody, my eyes are green and my hair is straight and dark brown like my dad's, who was essentially my mom's starter husband. In other words, I'm basically a living, breathing reminder of that giant mistake she made.

When the five of us go out together, I know I look more like the twins' babysitter than their stepsister. And that's how I get treated sometimes, too. As hired help—except I don't actually get paid. Taking care of the twins is something my mom makes me do for free because that's what big sisters do, she says. But why focus on that now, when I get to be Melody?

The blue pouch is labeled *sunscreen*. I unzip it, peek inside, and find the SPF 60 along with a note from Melody's mom: *Don't forget to reapply every hour and when you get out of the water. You'll thank me when you're my age. No one loves a prune face!*

She signed it *Love, Mom* with a happy face. I love the happy face. It's supercute and sweet.

I wonder why Melo never told me about the note or the sunscreen. Maybe she didn't want to rub in the fact that her mom is always so thoughtful, while my mom is so, well, not.

It's too bad because on the real first day of summer I ended up turning lobster red and it took me days to recover. The physical pain was bad enough, but then there was the annoyance of having to listen to my stepdad lecture me about the dangers of excess exposure to UV rays and the links between sunburn and skin cancer. Plus, I had to wear a giant floppy hat for the rest of the week and I look terrible in hats.

I will definitely make sure that Melody (in my body) applies the SPF 60, even though this is merely a dream. That's how good of a friend I am.

I'm about to tell her, but then I notice she's walking ahead of me.

"Hurry up," she calls, with a quick glance over her shoulder. Melody is walking fast, arms swinging, practically power walking like the grandmas in our neighborhood and looking just as ridiculous. All she's missing is the warm-up suit and the little pink two-pound weights.

I worry about my image for half a second but then remember that none of this actually matters. None of this is real. It's fantasyland and come to think of it, I should be having more fun.

Like, for instance, how cool would it be if this turned into one of those dreams where I could fly?

And who's to say it can't?

I jump up and thrust my arms into the air in my best imitation of Superman. I close my eyes and will myself to fly, but nothing happens.

"Um, what are you doing?" asks Melody. She's stopped in her tracks and looking at me as if I am crazy.

I don't blame her, but I also don't care.

"Purple spaghetti and flypaper sandwiches," I yell, since these are the first words that pop into my head.

I figure Melody will spew something equally ridiculous, or at least give me a double thumbs-up, but instead she looks at me all concerned and asks, "When are you going to accept that this is actually happening?"

"It can't be." I shake my head. Then I yell, "Fly," and leap toward the sky again. This time I throw my whole body forward.

I land in the sand, facedown.

Ouch.

My knee hurts. There's sand in my eye and it stings, badly. Also, it's not exactly dream pain, winking and theoretical and fuzzy around the edges. This pain is real. I rub my eyes except my fingers are sandy, too, so I only make things worse.

Aack!

As I climb to my feet I hear a familiar voice from behind me. "Hey, are you okay?"

I look back with my one good eye. Some surfer dude is running toward me. Except he's not just some surfer dude. He's Kevin.

"I'm fine," I say, brushing the sand off my elbows.

I'm not sure what to do next. Talking to Kevin always leaves me flustered.

He's closer now and he's got his wet suit only halfway

on, exposing a tanned, beautiful chest. "Um, that looked bad. Did you trip? Are you okay?"

Kevin is right next to me and we have never been this close. I am not about to tell him I injured myself while attempting to fly, so I stay silent. My eye is watering and it stings. I go to rub it, again, but Kevin grabs my hand.

"Wait, don't do that. You could scratch the cornea," he says. "You need to wash your eye out with fresh water. Hold on." He lets go of me, kneels, and starts rummaging through his backpack.

I stand there, stunned, my hand still warm from his touch.

Moments later he holds up a blue water bottle triumphantly. "Okay, sit down and tilt your head back and try to keep your eyes open," he explains as he unscrews the cap.

I do as he says and now my head is resting in his palm. I feel safe, taken care of. This is the best dream I have had in my whole entire life and I don't want to wake up. Not until a blast of ice-cold water squirts me right in the eye.

"Yikes!" I scream, and stand up, blinking and rubbing my eye furiously.

Kevin is laughing. "Hey, you weren't supposed to move. Remember?"

"You never told me that," I sputter. My face and hair are

sopping wet and my eye is sore, but the sting has been replaced by a dull ache. Much improved but not perfect.

"Sorry. Is it gone?"

"It's gone," I say, blinking. "Thank you. Um, you really know what you're doing."

"Yeah," he says, putting his water bottle away and zipping up his backpack. "I'm a volunteer EMT."

"A what?" I ask.

"An emergency medical technician," says Kevin, meeting my stunned gaze with a curious head tilt. "A junior one, anyway."

This information surprises me. "Really? That's, like, a thing?"

He laughs as he stands up and brushes the sand off his knees. "It is back in North Carolina."

"Oh, is that where you live?" I ask, shading my eyes with my hand, pretending like I don't already know.

He stares at me with this strange, uncertain smile and speaks to me as if I were a three-year-old child. "That's where I used to live, but now I'm in Braymar. I thought you knew—"

"Hey, that's where I live," I say, cutting him off.

"Did you hit your head on that fall, too?" he asks.

"Nope," I say. "Um, welcome to California. I'm Melody."

He looks at me like I've said something crazy. Except

I haven't—not since the purple spaghetti thing and no way could he have heard that.

"You are a trip, Melo," he says, as he picks up his surfboard and heads for the water.

My knees feel weak and not because they are bruised from my fall. Kevin has this effect on me.

I am confused by our conversation, and also by the fact that he knows my nickname. But I decide to let it go because dreams are weird and who cares when Kevin is so dreamy. It's funny describing someone as dreamy while I'm in a dream. Of course he's dreamy. This whole scene is. I watch his tan back fade into the distance, wondering if I should've kissed him while I had the chance.

"Are you ready to go?" Melody asks me, using my heart-shaped, sparkly glasses like a headband to pull back her hair. My hair. She's got one hand on her pushed-out hip, her elbow as sharp as the point of an extra-pointy knife. She seems nervous, but I don't know why.

"Sure," I say.

We settle on a spot about a hundred yards from the lifeguard stand. I spread out my towel, shrug out of my cardigan, and peel my sundress over my head. Normally I'm super self-conscious of my body. My legs are pale and scrawny and I have three moles the size of quarters by my left knee and they make me look part Dalmatian.

But in Melo's body I know I'm perfect—curvy and

narrow in all the right places. Tan, too. Even though her mom nags her about getting wrinkles, Melo is always so tan.

I stand there for a moment and admire my new body, which is clad in a navy blue one-piece. If I'm Melody tomorrow, I'm totally wearing a bikini.

I'm thinking this and staring down at my new boobs when I feel someone's eyes on me.

I look up. The lifeguard seems to be staring at me. I can't confirm this because he's wearing dark sunglasses and a big straw hat, but when he notices me noticing him he turns away, fast.

It feels strange, bordering on creepy, because the lifeguard, while cute, is way too old. But maybe I'm imagining things.

Melody is next to me and she's carefully inching her way out of my cutoffs. It's funny seeing my old self from this perspective.

Funny and disappointing.

She's wearing my brand-new red bikini. The triangle top is completely flat against her chest. It's cute, but not hot, which is disappointing because when I bought it back in May, I was going for hot. Sure, it looked only okay in the store but I figured at the beach with the sun shining down and the contrast of the bleached white sand and the blue water, it would really pop. And when I say *pop*, I mean, "make me look like a pop star." Except the suit does not pop. It makes her look much younger than twelve, especially with the heart-shaped glasses and fake diamond studs from Target. She looks like a little girl trying to dress like a teenager.

She could easily pass for an eight-year-old and I ache with embarrassment for my old self.

I also notice she's getting a little red in the face. "You should put on some sunscreen," I say, handing over the tube.

"If this is a dream, why do you care?" she asks, raising her eyebrows.

I laugh. "Good question. I'm not really sure, but it's better to be safe than sorry. And you'll thank me when you're old. No one loves a prune face."

Melody looks at me funny and then glances at my bag. "You read the note from my mom?" she asks, quietly.

"Yes," I say. "You're lucky she's so thoughtful."

Melody smirks and says, "That's one way to put it."

"What do you mean?" I ask.

Melody doesn't answer right away. Instead she lies down faceup and throws her arm over her eyes to protect them from the sun. "You'll see," she says finally.

* * *

When we ride through the tunnel at the end of our day, I make sure to keep my eyes wide open, to not wish for anything out loud or in my head. I like being Melody. I'd like to stay her for as long as possible. I don't want to wake up from this dream or have this wish canceled out on the return trip and I'm not taking any chances.

Kevin is not on the bus with us. We didn't see him at the beach again, either, so obviously he left while we were on our walk or at the snack bar.

Melody sits next to me and she's wearing the red-and-white-striped romper I bought on sale back in May. It seemed so cute and perfect for summer back when I tried it on. Yet seeing it from the outside, I realize I look like a candy cane, and not in a good way. My jean shorts have disappeared. I saw Melody forget to pack them and could've said something but decided I was doing her—and myself—a favor by letting them stay lost. Similarly, I shoved Melody's baggy cardigan into the bottom of her tote bag and am wearing the pink-and-white sundress without it.

My new motto is "If you've got it, flaunt it" and Melody has definitely got it. The sundress clings in all the right places without being clingy, necessarily.

As the beach bus pulls into the high school parking lot Melody says, "I'm hungry. Let's stop at the Golden Spoon on the way home." She's in a cheerful mood and she's not sunburned. I'm so proud of myself for pushing the sunscreen. I am an amazing friend.

"I'm always up for frozen yogurt," I say.

As soon as we get to the Golden Spoon, Melody marches forward and announces, "I'll have a half chocolate and half salted caramel with pretzel pieces and mochi, but please put the mochi on the bottom and the pretzels on top."

"Hey, that's my order!" I say.

"Duh, I know," says Melody, winking at me. "I'm you now."

Melody gets her yogurt from Vicki, the red-haired, high-ponytail-wearing lady who's always working behind the counter. After she pays she sits down at our usual table, right by the front door—in the sun, farthest from the bathrooms and closest to the outside without actually being outside because that's like eating in the parking lot.

I hang back, wondering if I have my taste buds or Melody's taste buds in this dream.

I decide to conduct an experiment. In my real life I can't stand plain tart yogurt, but since it's Melody's favorite flavor I ask for a sample.

When Vicki hands it over I'm surprised by how delicious it tastes. Refreshing, too.

As I'm finishing it, an older man walks into the yogurt

shop. He goes right to the counter but pauses when he sees me waiting to order.

"Go ahead," I tell him, my mouth half-filled with yogurt. "I'm not sure what I want."

"I'll wait," he says, giving me a friendly little wink. And he keeps staring even when I look away.

I wonder if I have yogurt somewhere on my face. I grab a napkin from the dispenser and wipe my chin, but when I look, I find it clean.

"Can I please try the salted caramel?" I ask. It's my favorite flavor in real life, but Melody never orders it.

Vicki nods from behind the counter and gives me a sample. I'm expecting to find it delicious and refreshing, except now it tastes disgusting—too sweet and too salty.

Looks like I'm Melody through and through, I think as I toss the tiny sample cup into the trash.

"I'll have a plain tart with marshmallows," I tell her. And something surprising happens when I say the word *marshmallow*. My mouth begins to water in anticipation. Melo really is crazy for them.

Vicki serves me my yogurt and says, "That'll be four dollars and ninety-five cents."

"Great." I pull out my wallet, open it, and panic. There's no cash inside, only a credit card. I never knew Melody had a credit card and I'm not sure what to do. What if Melody uses her credit card strictly for emergencies? I don't want to get her into trouble. I'm about to ask when I realize how silly this is. None of this is real. It's only a dream. I could go on a humongous shopping spree and none of it would matter because eventually I'm going to wake up.

I hand over the plastic. "Sorry, ten-dollar minimum," Vicki says with an apologetic smile.

It's surprising that there are charge card minimums in my dream. I turn to Melody. I had no extra money on the real first day of summer but I ask anyway, because maybe the dream-life details will be different.

Except Melody checks her wallet and tells me it's empty.

The man waiting sees what's going on and jumps forward. "I'll buy the yogurt for the young lady," he says, placing his hand on my back, up in between my shoulder blades.

His hand is warm and shocking. The sudden contact from a stranger seems odd. Wrong. Any strange guy touching me would rate extremely high in ick-factor, but this dude is old, as in dad-in-khaki-shorts-and-a-polo-shirt old.

I pull away. "No," I say. "You don't have to. I'll go without. It's no biggie."

"No, it would be my pleasure," he says, taking his hand off my back.

I'm glad he's not touching me anymore, but he's still smiling like we share a secret, which we most certainly do not.

I am tense, nervous. This isn't lifeguard attention, or Kevin attention. This is random-creepy-old-man attention and it's making me sick. I do not want the yogurt anymore, but Vicki is already handing it to me. And those marshmallows do look delectable. Thinking about them, my mouth waters all over again.

"Here you go," she says, brightly. She doesn't care. Or maybe she doesn't even notice the creep factor. This dude has given her a big tip and paid for my yogurt. Her job is done.

I take it. The man winks at me again and says, "My pleasure. How could I watch a pretty girl like you get deprived of frozen yogurt on such a beautiful day? It wouldn't be right."

I smile and mumble, "Thank you." My face is burning up, not just from embarrassment but from anger, too, because he shouldn't be talking to me like this. He shouldn't be watching me at all. It's weird and wrong.

"Anytime, sweetheart. You have the most beautiful eyelashes," he tells me, except he doesn't seem to be looking at my eyelashes. Now I'm getting why Melody always wore the cardigan with this dress and I kind of wish I had it on.

I want to inform this man that I'm only twelve and he's at least three times my age—probably more. He shouldn't be looking at me the way he is, but I don't say a word. Instead I go back to Melody.

"Are you okay?" she asks, giving me a knowing look.

"That was so weird," I whisper.

She nods, not surprised in the least bit.

Melody is always getting free stuff and lots of attention. It's just that from the outside it looks so easy and glamorous and awesome. Yet the attention from the old dude? So not awesome!

After yogurt we head on home and before I know it we're at the corner of Sycamore and Cherokee, where Melo and I always part ways. Normally she turns left and heads to the fancier part of town and I head right to the older, more run-down houses, the kind that don't have servants' quarters and wine cellars. But today everything is reversed.

"Good luck," says Melody.

"You, too," I say with a wave, and then head to Melody's humongous house at 21 Lynwood Court. It's behind large iron gates but I know the code, of course. It's 105—her mom's, Debbie's, weight when she got married.

As soon as I punch in the numbers the gates part, swift and soundless. I'd be lying if I said I wasn't excited.

Debbie's black Tesla is parked in the driveway. It's the

car Melo will probably get when she turns sixteen, as long as she keeps up her grades. I keep reminding her to study hard because it's not like I'm going to be handed a fancy sports car, or any car, for that matter. So I'll have to rely on her. Except Melody doesn't listen to me. School stuff doesn't come easy to her like it does to me, or to her older brother. Kyle got straight As in all honors classes in high school without even trying. He just finished his freshman year at Yale and is staying there for the summer to take extra classes for fun.

The exterior of the car is sleek and shiny, the inside buttery brown leather. I want to touch it but I refrain, because I know Debbie would notice my fingerprints. Two summers ago we decided to surprise Debbie and wash it, but she yelled at us for not drying it properly and leaving streaks.

Remembering that story makes me hope that Debbie isn't home. Except when I walk inside I can see all the way to the wall of windows at the back of the house. Debbie is doing squat thrusts around their gorgeous, black-bottomed pool. She's got a heavy-looking barbell on her shoulders.

Melo's mom is beautiful and her body is perfect. You know, for a mom. She looks a lot younger than my mom because she's already had a face-lift and she works out constantly and wears designer everything.

I am not sure what Melo does when she comes home on her own, like what their normal routine is, so I wander out to the pool and say hi. This seems like a good step, although my stomach flutters with nervousness because I'm worried Debbie will know something is up. Namely, that her daughter has disappeared and her best friend has taken over her body. It seems like the kind of thing a mother would notice.

"Hi, Mom," I say with a wave.

"Want to do sit-ups with me, sweetheart?" Debbie asks from the other end of the pool, midsquat.

"Um, no thanks," I say. "I'm tired."

She stops what she's doing, drops her barbell, and looks me up and down. "Oh, to be young again," she says. "To have that body and not have to work for it."

I'm not sure how to answer her, so I force a smile, give a little wave, and run upstairs.

I love Melody's room because it looks like it belongs in a magazine. And in fact, her whole house was featured in *Architectural Digest* a few years back, but Melody hates it when I remind her of that.

When I flop down on her bed I sink into the softest duvet cover in the world. It's light pink with turquoise stripes—Melody's favorite colors. The entire room was custom designed by Pierre, a decorator so famous he doesn't even need a last name. The bedspread matches the curtains, which match the wallpaper. Everything is color coordinated but with a mix of prints—stripes and polka dots and plaids—to make it more interesting. Melody has real oil paintings on her walls, mostly from the South of France. She and her family went on a big trip to Europe with the sole purpose of buying art for their house. She's not allowed to hang up her own stuff because anything not picked out by Pierre would "ruin the aesthetic," her mom told her. This drives Melody crazy, but I like how everything has a place and fits in perfectly and elegantly.

Anyone can hang up posters they find in the mall, but flying to another continent to shop for art is a big deal. Having your bedroom in a magazine is special. I've never understood why Melody doesn't see things that way.

I could get used to this fancy bed in this fancy room. I stretch out and yawn, exhausted. Sleep sounds delicious, but I fight to keep my eyes open. Next time I wake up, I'll probably be in my old body again, back to my own bland life, and a seventh grader, and I'm so not ready.

This could be my last moment as Melody, so I should take full advantage, do something bold. Maybe take the Tesla for a spin, or knock on Kevin's door and declare my love and infatuation. Or maybe just walk up to him and kiss him on the mouth without saying a word. I bring my fingertips to my lips, wondering how he'd react and what kissing actually feels like . . .

And right as those thoughts are forming in my head I hear Melo's phone chime with a new text:

Have fun at the beach?

The number on her screen is unfamiliar. I don't even recognize the area code. There's no name attached, only the letter *K*. I figure the message must be from Melo's brother, Kyle.

Yup! How's school? I type back.

Huh? K replies.

That's weird. I type: **Kyle?**

The reply comes back: **NOPE**

Who is this? I ask.

You're funny, K writes back.

Totally confused. Are you trying to reach Melody or is this a wrong number? I ask.

The response doesn't come right away. And once it does it leaves me even more confused.

How hard did you hit your head during that fall?

I think back to my flying attempt. Is that the fall Kyle is referring to? It has to be. But how could he know, unless he's not Kyle? But who could he be?

Who is this? I ask again.

Instead of a name I see a bunch of happy face emoticons: ☺ ☺ ☺ ☺

Well, Kyle is a genius but he always was a little odd. This must be the part of my dream where things stop making sense. Like, maybe next thing I know a bird will fly in the window and start singing opera. I toss the phone aside and rub my eyes, unable to muster the energy to get off the bed, or to fight sleep any longer. It's been fun being Melody but this dream is getting trippy and anyway, I can't keep my eyes open. *Goodbye perfect life,* I think as I drift off to sleep.

Except the next thing I know I'm being shaken awake.

"I believe you've gotten enough beauty sleep," Melody's mom says.

I open my eyes and see Debbie up close. Her hair has been styled into a sleek blond bob and she's wearing huge glittery diamond hoops. Her fancy silver ball gown rustles as she balances on the highest, most painful-looking stilettos I've ever seen.

"Debbie!" I say, as I scramble to sit up in bed.

I don't know why I'm here, where Melody is, or what is going on.

Melody's mom looks at me like I'm crazy. "Since when do you call me Debbie?"

Um, since we met when I was in kindergarten and you told me you were too young to go by Mrs. Marshall, is what I'm thinking, but I don't say it yet. I'm too flustered. Instead I blink and rub my eyes and—wait a minute. Why am I wearing pink polka-dotted nail polish? Oh yeah, I'm still in the dream, still Melody. "Sorry, Mom," I say. "I'm hardly awake."

Luckily, Debbie doesn't dwell on my mistake because she has another agenda. "Please don't wear your smelly flip-flops in bed. This duvet cost a small fortune and now I've got to get it dry-cleaned."

"Sorry," I say, kicking off my sandals.

"I unpacked for you," she says, holding a little pink pouch in my face, "and I noticed you didn't eat your snack."

"Melody and I got nachos," I say, rubbing my eyes, still trying to figure things out.

Then, when Debbie continues to stare at me, I say, "I mean Katie and me. Katie and me got nachos. Katie and I, that is."

For some reason she still looks horrified. "You ate nachos?" she asks. Except *nachos* comes out like it's a dirty word.

I nod, cautiously, thinking maybe opera-singing birds would be less bizarre than this conversation.

Debbie shakes her head. "You've really got to be more careful. You think you can eat whatever you want, but the older you get, the harder it's going to be."

"The harder what's going to be?" I ask, curious.

"Stop being difficult," snaps Debbie as she heads for

the door. "I'm going out tonight. I left you a salad in the fridge. Be careful with the dressing. It's nonfat, but there's still sugar in it so don't use too much. Especially after your splurge at the beach."

"Okay," I reply meekly, wondering when Melody's mom got so crazy, and feeling grateful that she's at least going out tonight.

I hide in Melody's room until I hear the creak of the gates opening and Debbie's car speeding out of the driveway. Then I head downstairs and eat the salad. Still feeling hungry, I order a pizza. And luckily the place takes credit cards, since I can't find any cash.

Once I finish I'm not sure what to do, which is bizarre because I'm always at Melody's. When my mom and Jeff went on their honeymoon in Hawaii, I got to stay with Melody for ten whole days and we had the most amazing time. But being in the house alone is kinda creepy. The Marrakesh tile, hand painted and imported from Morocco, feels cool on my bare feet. The hallways are so empty that my voice echoes. I play pinball in the game room. I watch some reality TV in the screening room. Then I paint Melody's toenails, each one a different color of the rainbow.

Eventually I wander back upstairs to Melody's room. I decide to go through her closet, pick out something to wear in case I get another day at the beach as Melo. And

I hope I do because it was fun, for the most part. Except every single one of Melody's bathing suits is dark and drab.

I head to Debbie's closet instead, which used to be a bedroom. Sailing in through the door, I realize I have hit the jackpot. The closet is humongous and it's filled with racks and racks of the most fabulous clothing I have ever laid eyes on. Debbie has an entire section devoted to bathing suits and beachwear and that's where I gravitate. It only takes a few seconds to find my favorite—a gold-and-white-striped V-neck one-piece with a large cutout on each side. It fits me perfectly and looks amazing with Debbie's sheer white cover-up. I head over to her wall of shoes and select a pair of gold high-heel sandals. They, too, fit as if they were made for my feet.

With the look complete, I stare at myself in the mirror from every angle, piling my curls on top of my head and then letting them fall down again.

I look absolutely irresistible. Like I could seriously model, if I wanted to.

Hmmm . . . thinking about modeling makes me think of fashion shows and how fun it would be to have my own private one right now, since Debbie's fabulous wardrobe is literally at my fingertips. I step out of the heels, shrug out of the cover-up, and take off the bathing suit. I try on a silver-sequined ball gown, then a black lace one with a zipper that goes all the way up the back, and then an emerald-green sheath. Next I try on Debbie's designer jeans and knee-high boots and a variety of sweaters and silky tops and tanks. I keep going and soon stumble upon the most gorgeous red minidress I have ever seen. I put it on immediately, and then find some matching red stilettos.

I look amazing, but there's room for improvement. I head to Debbie's vanity and put on some makeup.

As I am admiring my stunning reflection in the full-length mirror I hear a knock on the door. Someone is here. I kick off the heels because they're too high to actually walk in and hurry downstairs. When I look through the peephole I see Kevin standing on the front stoop.

My heart does that flippy thing again as I open the door.

"Hi," I say, confused as ever that he's here. Because we only just met this morning at the beach. He's not supposed to know he lives on the same street as Melody.

Except obviously Kevin does know. Because he doesn't say hi back. Instead, he gives me this sweet little smile and leans in and kisses me.

MELODY

Being a Miller!

The sun is sinking below the mountain peaks in the distance. It's my favorite time of day: dusk, right before darkness makes its sneaky, creepy descent. The sky glows warm and fuzzy. No one's in a hurry at six o'clock. Everything is quiet and mellow, as if the whole world is wrapped in a big fuzzy blanket.

Katie's house stands in front of me, quaint and brick and two stories high with three cozy bedrooms upstairs. As I walk up the path to the front door, I smell sweet herbs. The giant terra-cotta pots on either side of me overflow with basil and violet, spearmint and thyme. I know because we helped her mom plant them one Saturday in the spring.

Ryan and Reese were there, too. When Ryan had to go

inside to use the bathroom, he didn't take off his shoes like he was supposed to, and he tracked in mud, but Katie's mom didn't scream and yell. She didn't even raise her voice.

Instead she simply had a nice talk with Ryan, explaining why she'd asked him to remove his shoes in the first place—to avoid this messy scenario. Then she helped him get a rag and soap and a bucket of water and she showed him how to clean it up himself, which he did without complaint.

Last time I tracked mud in my house my mom screamed at me and then called for Greta, the weekend maid, and made me apologize to her for making more work, which was humiliating because Greta wouldn't even look me in the eye. Then later I caught her staring at me with a pitying glance.

But dwelling on the past is like scribbling storm clouds on a perfectly sunny picture. There's no need and no point because everything is different now. I'm a different person, better and luckier. I need to enjoy it while I can— for this whole entire summer—because that's what I wished for: to start the summer over as Katie. And here I am. It's happening and it will continue to happen. It's got to.

I raise my fist and am about to knock on the front door out of habit when I realize I don't have to. I belong here and I even have my own key. I hope. Katie is always losing her key, so with a rising sense of dread I take her backpack off my back and unzip the front pocket.

Yikes! Everything spills out before I can stop it: crumpled tissues, a Rubik's Cube, a pad of paper and three purple pens, an orange highlighter, and a blue hair band. Also, my silver hoop earrings—the ones I loaned her back in March and haven't seen since. Katie claimed they vanished and I know she wasn't lying. Lots of things vanish in Katie's world. Katie is the most unorganized person I know. It's pretty annoying but I guess I can help her now. Help myself, that is. After I put on the earrings, I reach for the special hook where Katie's key is supposed to be clipped but it's not there. Of course it's not there.

I groan out of frustration at Katie. Even though she acts like she's got the world figured out, her room and her backpack and everything else on the inside are a mess. It drives me bananas.

I stuff her things back into her bag, vowing to put them in their proper place later on tonight. Then I zip the bag shut and open up the main section to finally find the key at the very bottom—along with five quarters and three pennies—all of which I deposit in her Hello Kitty change purse. A change purse I got her for her birthday last year in an attempt to get her more organized. It's empty, which is so typical. If Katie were here

I'd ask, "Do you like digging around the dregs of your backpack for quarters when you're trying to buy a juice at lunch?"

And she would roll her eyes and say, "Melo, it's not good to be so rigid," or something like that, except I don't need to worry about that because she's not here. Not really, anyway. I'm Katie!

I feel lighter and happier and jumpier every time I say the words, even quietly to myself in my own head. Katie's head. Ha ha!

I'm Katie I'm Katie I'm Katie. I'm smart and funny and regular-looking—cute, even, but not too cute that everyone is always fawning over me like my looks are the only things that matter. Like that's *all* I am.

But better than being Katie is that Katie's family is now my family. I've got cool parents who actually pay attention to me, and two awesome kid brothers.

After forcing the smile off my face, I unlock the door and step inside.

To my left is the living room, which has been taken over by Ryan and Reese. Lego bricks and Matchbox cars are everywhere and a gigantic blue racetrack extends from one corner to the other. There's also a drum set and a guitar and an old, beat-up piano that Katie knows how to play. She's been taking lessons since she was four years old.

"Daddy!" I hear from two darling little voices as the boys race toward the door.

"Nope. It's just Katie," I say to Ryan and Reese, who skid to a stop when they see me.

It's hard to keep from falling to my knees and giving them gigantic hugs. Ryan and Reese are my favorite kids in the whole entire world, both sweet and adorable with their reddish-blond hair and bright blue eyes. They are not identical twins, though. Ryan is a little taller and his nose turns up and he doesn't have as many freckles as Reese, whose hair is stick straight. Ryan's is wavy. Plus, Ryan is always picking his nose and Reese bites his nails. Katie claims to not be able to tell them apart but I think it's an act. They really are their own kids, distinct and amazing.

Reese seems disappointed I'm not their dad. His hands go to his mouth as he gnaws at his thumbnail. Ryan grins at me, bashfully. He worships Katie, follows her silently with his big blue eyes whenever they're in the same room. Not that she notices.

"What are you guys up to?" I ask brightly as I drop my backpack at the foot of the steps.

"Reese made a car but he won't share it," Ryan says with a pout.

"Ryan didn't share his plane yesterday," Reese says.

"That's because you always break them!" Ryan cries, finger inching toward his nose.

"I was trying to fly it," says Reese, stomping his foot. Reese is a big foot stomper. "That's what planes are for."

"Not Lego planes. Plus, your fingers are always wet!" yells Ryan.

He has a point but I don't say so. Neither does Reese, except he does quickly remove his pinky from his mouth. Then he turns around and bolts upstairs.

"Wait for me!" Ryan calls, scrambling after him.

I am left in their wake, along with the faint smell of sweet-and-sticky boy. I inhale deeply. Katie is so lucky. She has no idea. What a great thing to come home to every day—the energy and passion and warmth of two lively people who actually want to see you.

My house is always so cold and empty, my footsteps echo when I walk.

"Katie, is that you?" Katie's mom is calling from the kitchen.

"Yes," I reply, my voice wavering. I want to address Katie's mom by her name, Anya, like I usually do, but of course I can't. "Yes, Mother. I'm here," I add. Katie's been calling her mom "Mother" ever since her parents got divorced. It sounds weird coming from my lips—too stiff and formal. Of course, it sounds weird when Katie says it, too. She's still so mad that her parents split up even though it happened years ago. I mean, yeah, it's got to be hard but guess what? Katie still has two parents who love her a lot and now they don't spend all their time fighting.

There's no tension in her house. Everyone has moved on and is happy with their lives. And Katie has two homes with two awesome stepparents and two new brothers to boot. That's so much better than having parents who stay married for the sake of appearances, parents who don't even speak to each other, but that's another story. One I don't have to live in right now because I'm Katie!

Let's just hope everyone sees me that way. Because as excited as I am about this whole body-switching thing, I can't hide my nervousness. I'm worried Katie's mom will recognize me as the impostor that I am. And then what happens?

Of course, if I fooled Katie, then I'm sure I could fool her mom.

This is what I tell myself as I stroll into the kitchen, where Anya is unloading the dishwasher.

"Hi there!" I say, still surprised that my voice sounds so much like Katie's—high-pitched and sharp around the edges. Her words escape her mouth in a clipped tone, like she's not wasting any time.

Katie's mom's hair is pulled back in a loose bun. Red strands have escaped, framing her narrow freckled face. She's sweaty and flushed. If she were wearing makeup it would be running, but Katie's mom never wears makeup. My mom, on the other hand, is obsessed with makeup.

She will not leave the house without it. Actually, she will not leave her bedroom without it.

I've figured out that there are moms who transform themselves and moms who go out into the world declaring *this is me*. My mom is all about covering up the truth, and I'm not just talking about her wrinkles.

Funny thing is, my mom and Katie's weren't always so different. They used to be great friends. That's how Katie and I met. We went to nursery school together and we had playdates every week.

I've seen old pictures of my mom and Anya, both of them in yoga pants and tank tops, their hair in loose ponytails. It's like they started at the same point but Katie's mom went in one direction and mine in the other.

"How was the beach?" Anya asks, like she's really interested in the answer.

"Amazing!" I say, trying not to grin too widely because I'm still feeling amazed. The beach was life altering, which I could add but don't because, duh, this is a secret.

"Glad you girls had fun," she says, smiling sweetly. "How's Melody?"

"Good," I say with a shrug, wondering why she's asking. "Great."

"Are you sure?" she asks. My spidey-senses tell me this is a leading question. Problem is, I don't know where she's going with it. Why would Katie's mom be so interested in me?

"Why do you ask?" I wonder.

She looks at me strangely and I start to panic, like she must know something's up. Obviously they had some conversation about me, meaning Melody, that they are privy to and I'm not. I should just go along with things, pretend I know what's what. Be cooler than I am about this whole thing and act more confident like Katie would.

But it's too late. My cheeks feel warm as Anya tilts her head to one side and stares at me, appraising. She opens her mouth like she's about to ask me another question, but before she does, we hear the door open again and this time it's Ryan and Reese's dad, Jeff.

The boys scream as they scramble down the steps, cheering and tripping over each other like puppies, both desperate for their dad's attention.

Anya and I look at each other and grin and then we both wander into the living room.

Reese and Ryan are ordering Jeff to sit down and listen to their concert. He flops down on the couch, cheerfully, and pushes back his wavy blond hair to reveal warm dark eyes. He's in jeans and a blue-and-white-checked shirt.

Reese is on drums. Ryan plays the recorder. The

combined sound is horrific and at the same time wonderful—music to my brand-new ears.

I feel as if I'm in the middle of a sitcom. Except not the kind where the parents are always fighting and the kids are bratty and filled with snarky comments and everyone's up to no good. I mean the last three minutes of every sitcom, where everyone gets along and is nice and loving and the hijinks are over, the misunderstandings resolved: a shiny, perfect, happy family.

After listening to the boys' show, Jeff gives them a standing ovation.

"That was amazing, guys," Anya says.

Jeff kisses Anya hello, then hands her a loaf of bread. "It's fresh from the farmer's market."

"Oh, and still warm," says Anya, truly pleased.

Jeff says hi to me and asks me how my day was.

"Dad, you're not listening!" Reese yells.

"I have been listening, but now I need to help with dinner," Jeff explains, laughing good-naturedly. "I promise I can hear you from every room in the house."

"That's good, right, Daddy?" asks Ryan.

"It's perfect," says Jeff, kissing the top of his head.

I follow him and Anya into the kitchen, all of us wanting to escape the noise but not saying so.

As Jeff heads to the center island he rolls up his sleeves, revealing the *Emily* tattoo on his right forearm. Emily was the name of his first wife, the twins' mom, who died when the boys were barely a year old.

I try not to stare at the tattoo when I see him but it's hard not to notice. It's large and the letters are in fancy cursive with a garland of flowers surrounding her name. He rubs it absentmindedly on occasion. I've noticed Katie's mom looking at it, too. I wonder what that's like. Knowing there was someone important before you. Before and after you, that is. Katie's mom and Jeff dated when they were in the sixth grade, and then broke up when his family moved away, only to meet up again years later. It's weird to think about.

I can't imagine wanting to marry any boy I know, including the one I'm secretly dating. But I don't need to think about that now. Not when this is the beginning of summer, and not my problem anymore. I'm not the one who's secretly dating Kevin. Katie is.

I wonder if she's figured it out yet. That'll be interesting . . .

I wonder if she realizes this is real, that we've actually switched bodies. Knowing Katie, she probably still thinks this whole thing is a dream. She doesn't believe in anything she can't see. We're different like that. And obviously I'm right.

"So you never answered me. How was your day?" Jeff asks. I mean Jeff asks Katie. Me. How would Katie answer this question?

"Great," I say, and because Katie's answers are never that simple I add, "Melody and I went to the beach and it was pretty foggy, actually. Not what I was expecting. And the bus was crowded, too."

"I hope you were still careful with the sunscreen," he says.

There's a lot of talk about sunscreen in Katie's house because Emily died of cancer. Plus, Jeff is an environmental scientist. He's a professor at one of the nearby colleges, Cal State Northridge.

"I was," I say, rolling my eyes like I knew Katie would. "You don't always have to remind me, you know . . ."

Suddenly there's yelling from the living room. Reese and Ryan are fighting about whose turn it is to sleep on the top bunk. They switch off nightly yet can never keep track. Jeff sighs and Anya puts down her knife. "I'll handle them if you finish cooking," she says.

"That's the best offer I've had all day," Jeff replies.

Once Anya leaves, Jeff turns to me and says, "Okay, sport. Want to help with dinner?"

It seems like I can't say no. Katie wouldn't, I don't think. And anyway, I don't want to. "Sure, why not?"

He surveys the kitchen island. "Looks like we're having veggie burgers and salad. You can chop the carrots."

"Okay," I say, moving to the left so I'm standing in front of the cutting board. I'm not sure what to do from there—I don't help with the cooking at home.

We don't actually do a lot of cooking at home. Family dinners only happen on holidays and we get those meals catered. On the rare instance that my dad is in town he has work dinners and my mom usually joins him. Other times they have benefits and parties to attend. And when my mom is at home, when it's only the two of us, well, she doesn't exactly eat. Instead she juices vegetables into some murky bitter concoction and gulps it down. She's tried to get me to do the same but I refuse. So she relents and serves me food delivered from some health food place.

The actual cooking of a real meal is unfamiliar and I'm not prepared. I feel queasy as Jeff hands me four fat carrots. I take them and set them down and then stare at them for too long, wondering where to start. I've no idea, which makes me want to cry. But I can't because Katie would never cry. Not over carrots. Also, Katie would chop them however she wanted to and if someone argued she'd say, "That's the way it's supposed to be done."

I need to be more like Katie. This isn't only about living in her house and getting to hang out with her family. I'm here in her body so I can learn to be more like her. That's what I want and that's what I need. Especially now that middle school is right around the corner.

I take a deep breath and pick up a knife and set the carrot down, awkwardly, on the cutting board. I raise the knife and freeze, my body rigid with panic because I don't want to mess this up.

But how am I supposed to cut the carrots when there are so many options? How does Katie do this and why haven't I paid attention in the past?

Would she cut carrots into sticks or into little circles like nickels, except tastier? And if I am supposed to do circles, how thick should they be? Ryan and Reese are still pretty young. What if they choke on my carrot nickels? I took CPR in gym but I'm afraid to administer it in real life. I know I'll mess things up and Ryan and Reese will get hurt or worse and then I'll never forgive myself.

I try to remember dinner at Katie's house in the past. I've been here a million times, so it shouldn't be this hard. Except I never paid attention to the shape of the carrots. Now that voice inside my head is calling me stupid because why didn't I notice the right way? How could I have been so unobservant? Why didn't I know that one day I'd be making dinner in Katie's kitchen in front of Katie's stepdad and inside of Katie's body and I'd be expected to know better? I should've been prepared for this scenario.

I feel like I'm in school and my teacher has just called

on me and of course I've been daydreaming. That happened constantly in Ms. Jaffe's class last year and the worst part was always the look in her eyes—the distinct blend of disappointment and concern. She never said so but I know what she was always wondering: *Why isn't Melody smart like her brother? Did Kyle get the smart genes? Or is she just lazy? Her best friend, Katie, is bright. I wonder what the two of them have in common . . .*

"Something wrong, Katie?" asks Jeff.

I blink to snap myself out of my daze and shake my head. "Nope. Everything's great!"

Then I start cutting the carrots into nickel-size pieces, about a quarter of an inch thick. I'll cut them in half after that so nobody chokes, and I'm feeling pretty good about my plan.

Except Jeff is still looking at me funny.

"What?" I ask.

"You might want to peel that carrot first," he says, handing me the peeler.

"Right," I say, coughing. "Of course."

Maybe my teachers are right. Maybe I'm simply not smart enough.

I dump the unpeeled slices into the compost box in the corner and get to work at the sink, peeling the remaining three carrots.

I make sure to take my time with the cutting. I don't

want another job because that would mean another opportunity to mess things up.

"Those look great. Thanks, honey," Jeff says, sweeping the carrot pieces into the salad bowl.

My plan worked. Jeff is happy and I am, too, and the twins are building Lego rocket ships quietly in the den. Dinner is ready and soon we're at the dining room table. The burgers are displayed on a blue platter that Katie painted by hand at Color Me Lovely, this ceramics store at the mall that we used to visit when we were younger. I know because I was there when she painted it. It's got a chip in one side and I think it's so cool that they still use it. It has such sentimental value they're not going to throw it away. Katie's mom and Jeff sit at either end of the table. The twins are next to each other on one side and I sit across from them on the other.

Ryan is picking his nose.

Reese bites his pinky nail.

I am trying not to smile too hard because I don't want to arouse suspicion. But it's hard because there is no place I'd rather be right now. No one I'd rather be than Katie.

As Jeff pours both of the twins milk he says, "Please go wash your hands, guys."

Both boys grumble but scrape back their chairs and get up from the table. We hear them squabble over who gets to go first and then they are back, wiping their wet hands on their shorts.

Reese eyes the milk and says, "He has more than me!"

Reese is always thinking Ryan has more.

"No, it's perfectly even," Jeff tells them. "Want me to get the scale so we can weigh it?"

"Yes," says Reese.

Jeff actually gets up and comes back with a tiny portable kitchen scale, like weighing drinks is something that happens every single night around here. Maybe it does. Except Ryan has already guzzled his milk.

"No fair," Reese cries, once he realizes. "He destroyed the evidence."

Ryan burps. "I didn't destroy it, I drank it."

"That's the same thing!" Reese argues.

"It's fine, boys. There's plenty of milk for everyone," says Anya.

Reese drains his milk and asks for more and then Ryan burps and Reese grabs his plate and moves to the other end of the table.

"I'm sitting next to Katie," he says. "It's too yucky over there."

"You're too yucky," Ryan says as he sticks out his tongue.

"Hey, no one is yucky," says Jeff. "Let's everyone get along tonight."

I try some salad. It's delicious, especially the carrots.

"When are you and Melo taking us to the beach?" Reese asks me.

"Yeah, when?" Ryan repeats. "Melody promised us."

I want to tell them we'd go tomorrow, but I'm nervous that Jeff and Anya will know something's up. They must notice that I'm not acting like myself.

What would happen if they found out Katie and I did the whole body-switch? They wouldn't believe it, probably, and I don't blame them. If I told them, they'd think their daughter had gone crazy. Maybe they'd take me to the doctor. I don't want to go to the doctor. Doctors mean shots and cold hands pressing into your tummy, and forcing you to say ah so they can gag you with their tongue depressor. So instead I make a face at them, in my perfect imitation of Katie. "Talk to Melody. It was her idea to take you!" I cringe at how horrible I sound. But this is how Katie talks to her stepbrothers.

Out of the corner of my eye I catch Jeff and Anya sharing a knowing glance: secret parent language. This is how I know I'm pulling it off. They look disappointed but not suspicious. I feel bad for being rude to Ryan and Reese, but I have no choice. That's what Katie would do.

"Call her and I'll ask her," says Ryan.

"I'll call. What's her number?" Reese is getting up and heading to the phone.

"Everyone sit down and no phones at the table," says Jeff.

Reese flops back down in his seat and says, "After dinner then."

"Maybe," I say. "Melody is pretty busy tonight."

I wonder what Katie's doing. Probably wandering around my house alone. My dad is in San Francisco, as usual, and my mom probably has something else going on—a benefit or board meeting or cocktail party. She'd rather do anything than stay at home with me and I don't totally blame her. Our house is cold and lonely, especially now with Kyle away. Katie isn't used to being by herself and I'm sure it's driving her crazy. She's always complaining about the lack of privacy in her house, ever since Jeff and the twins moved in. She doesn't know what true solitude is about. How lonely life can be when everyone in your family wants to be somewhere else—and usually is.

She doesn't appreciate how amazing her life is. Because being here with the Millers at the dinner table? It's awesome.

The food is hot and delicious and there's lots of it and everyone is eating. The table is crowded—half the size of our dining room table at home, which is ironic because there's hardly ever more than two people at ours.

"Did you hear about the exploding Eelons?" Jeff asks.

"The what?" Ryan asks.

"The Eelon is an electric car and some of the batteries have been catching fire," Jeff explains.

"Is that the car that Melody's dad has?" Ryan asks. "The fancy one with the third row?"

"Yes," I say. Not only does my dad have a Eelon, his company supplies some of its parts. So I'm a little concerned. "What do you mean they're catching on fire?"

"There's a big piece in today's *LA Times*," Anya tells me, seeming surprised. "You didn't see it?"

I shrug, not realizing that Katie is expected to read the newspaper. "I was in a hurry this morning. Must've missed it."

"Yeah, going to the beach without us!" says Ryan.

Jeff swallows a bite of veggie burger and says, "When they go too fast, the batteries overheat and they can spark and actually catch on fire. It's happened twice this month."

"That's terrible," says Anya. "I was so excited about the new technology."

"Well, the whole existence of the electric car in general raises some interesting moral questions," Jeff says.

I'm surprised Jeff is criticizing electric cars since he's an environmental scientist.

"Aren't you supposed to be happy about electric cars?" I ask. "Isn't it so much better for the environment not to have a bunch of gas-guzzling cars around? That's what my—I mean, that's what Melody's dad says."

"It would be wonderful if everyone drove electric cars," says Jeff. "But that's not possible for most people because they're so expensive. Only wealthier people can afford them, and they get to save on gas plus they're given tax credits, so essentially there's an incentive program that benefits the rich."

I think about this for a moment. "I guess it would be better if someone could invent something to turn gas-guzzling cars into electric cars automatically. Rather than making people buy brand-new cars."

Jeff points his fork at me and smiles. "That's an excellent point, Katie. You should invent something like that."

I sit up straighter in my chair. Maybe I can handle dinner at the Millers'. I seem to be keeping up. Maybe it's being in Katie's body. People expect me to be smart and thoughtful, so I am. Whatever I say, I'm given the benefit of the doubt because everyone knows Katie is a smarty-pants.

If I were Melody, on the other hand . . . that's a different story.

As I'm thinking this I suddenly feel something cold and wet on my lap. "Ah!" I yell, surprised. I look down. Ryan is looking sheepish and for good reason: he's spilled his entire glass of milk on me. A particularly impressive feat considering I am all the way on the other side of the table.

"Sorry," says Ryan.

He looks as if he's about to cry. It's the sweetest, saddest thing I've seen all night. "Don't worry, Ryan." I start to get up, thinking I'll give him a quick hug, but stop.

The entire table goes silent.

Everyone stares at me in surprise.

Uh-oh. This is clearly not a Katie reaction. I sit back down and bark, "Ryan, will you quit acting so clumsy? You are so annoying."

"Sorry," he says again, rubbing his eyes, holding in tears.

I feel terrible but at least I'm staying in character.

Anya gets up and runs to the kitchen, coming back moments later with a dish towel.

I mop the milk off my clothes, trying to seem annoyed. I'll have to change out of the romper, but this isn't actually a bad thing. I'd never say so because I don't want to hurt the real Katie's feelings, but she makes some odd fashion choices. And by odd I actually mean terrible.

"Be right back," I say, heading upstairs to change into jeans and a T-shirt.

When I return to the table, everyone is finished eating.

"Can we please be excused?" asks Reese, speaking for himself and his brother.

"Sure," says Anya.

"Me, too?" I ask, standing up to clear my plate.

Jeff says he'll do the dishes. I'm about to follow the twins upstairs when Anya reminds me it's time to practice the piano.

"Twenty minutes," she says, pointing to her watch.

I gaze at the piano standing in the corner of the den. Katie has to practice for twenty minutes every single day. She complains about it all the time but the cool thing is she's really good. I love listening to Katie play the piano.

Gulping, I slowly walk over to the piano and sit down on the bench. Then I look down at my skinny, pale, freckled hands, wondering where piano-playing ability comes from. Is it all in the fingers? I hope so. With every fiber of my being I hope I've been given not just Katie's eyes and hair and nose and mouth and voice and freckles and skin and each bone in her body, but her musical gifts, too.

If not, well, then this could be the end of the charade.

KATIE

Kissing Confusion

I kissed a real, live boy and not just any boy—I kissed my biggest crush in the whole entire universe. He was my first choice of boy, my only choice: Kevin!

Being Melody is even more amazing than I ever imagined. If I were Katie right now I'd be practicing piano. But instead I'm here with the most gorgeous guy in town.

I am so blown away by this fact that I cannot think of anything to say, even though he's standing right in front of me.

This is the best dream I have ever had in my whole entire life.

Better than that time I dreamed I was opening for Lorde at the Hollywood Bowl. Better even than the time I dreamed that Lorde was opening for me.

Because guess what? Kevin is still standing here.

I wish I could float up out of my body and watch this scene from across the room. I wish I'd taken a selfie of us kissing on my phone. Then I'd have it forever and could use it as my screen saver. Except it would be Melody's face, not mine. For the moment, though, I push that small fact out of my mind and focus on Kevin.

He smells like sunscreen and sweat and something vaguely fruity. Cherry-flavored ChapStick, I think.

Yes, it definitely is.

I didn't know Kevin used ChapStick. And cherry flavored? This surprises me. He doesn't seem like the type. No guy does, really. But this makes me like Kevin even more. How funny and unpredictable he is. It's almost too adorable.

Although a bit odd.

Not odd in a bad way, I don't think. Normally I associate cherry-flavored ChapStick with this girl Rebecca from my old Girl Scout troop. She always wore her hair in braids and sucked on the tips, making them wet and pointy and kind of fruity smelling.

But why am I thinking about braid-sucking Girl Scouts when I'm gorgeous and in Melody's gorgeous house, wearing her mom's gorgeous red dress? I'm standing next to Kevin and he's gorgeous, too. Are you sensing a theme here?

Today is amazing.

What better way to top it off? Like the cherry on top of a sundae with extra whipped cream. No, better than a simple cherry. This is like a whole extra sundae or a cherry-flavored ChapStick kiss.

I'm waiting for Kevin to gaze, lovingly, into my eyes, to tell me how amazingly perfect and smart and wonderful I am. The answer to his hopes and dreams. Maybe he'll suggest a walk around the neighborhood. We'll hold hands as we head down the street and maybe stumble upon an abandoned litter of puppies, which we will rescue and feed milk to with an eyedropper.

I wonder if Melody still has that bicycle built for two in her garage. Maybe we can break it out tomorrow, if there is a tomorrow in my dream. I sure hope it lasts longer than this one day.

Wait a second. Why did Kevin kiss Melody when it's the first day of summer?

According to my memory, which is excellent by the way, Melody and I *saw* Kevin for the first time on the first day of summer. That's when I finally worked up the nerve to approach him. Melody was with me at the time, of course. We're always together. And I introduced the two of them, because I'm nice like that, and had no idea she'd betray me. Anyway, my point is, we both met him for the first time then.

Except the Fourth of July is in the future—weeks away!

Why would Kevin kiss me if we don't even know each other?

In what universe does this make sense?

Kevin smiles and asks, "Can I come in?"

"Huh?" I ask. "Oh yeah. Sure." He comes in and we walk into the living room and sit down on the couch. Good.

This is better than I'd imagined. This is Kevin, the man of my dreams.

And this is a dream.

Isn't it?

Of course it's a dream.

It has to be.

People don't switch bodies in real life. It's impossible.

Except, so far in my dream, practically every single detail checks out, meaning everything is grounded in reality.

Melody's mom looks and sounds and acts exactly like Melody's mom.

Vicki and the icky old dude at the Golden Spoon are the same.

I can't fly.

I feel pain.

I love the taste of plain tart yogurt.

I am Melody through and through. My mouth waters at the mere mention of the word *marshmallow*.

And speaking of mouths . . . why was this one on

mine, when it's the first day of summer? Why did Kevin walk in here like he's been here a million times before? Is time bending? Am I now at the end of summer? No. Something tells me there's a more logical explanation.

I need to hear it, so I turn to Kevin.

Part of me doesn't want to ask the question, because I don't want to ruin this perfect moment, but I need to know the truth.

I tilt my head and give Kevin a sideways glance. "Hey, what day is it?" I ask.

"What do you mean?" he asks.

"I mean today. What day is it?"

He looks at me blankly. "Um, Monday?"

"Right, Monday, as in the first day of summer."

"Oh, yeah," he says, sitting back. "Of course it is." He laughs and runs his fingers through his hair. "Did I do okay at the beach? Pretending to meet you for the first time? You were acting so funny. I couldn't figure out why, at first, but then I realized it was an act to throw Katie off, and you did an amazing job. She seemed thoroughly confused. No way could she have a clue about us."

Yikes! Hearing these words, replaying the afternoon in my head, I feel sick inside.

I don't want to ask this next question but I have to. "If today's the first day of summer, then how long have we known each other?" I wonder.

Kevin doesn't answer me right away and at this point, he almost doesn't have to. I can tell by the look in his eyes that I'm not going to like what I hear.

"It was over Christmas break, remember? Are you sure you're feeling okay? Because confusion could be a symptom of a concussion, and I didn't think you hit your head when you fell this morning, but maybe you did and—"

"No, I'm fine," I say, sinking back into the couch cushions.

The truth hits me like a lightning bolt straight to my aching heart. Melody was right. This is no dream.

We've switched bodies for real. My wish came true. I'm starting summer over as Melody. This is really happening, and that's not all.

When I spied Melody and Kevin kissing in her hot tub, I was furious because she stole him away from me. We got in a huge fight because I fell for Kevin first and we both agreed that I could have him.

Except I was wrong about that. Melody actually knew Kevin way before I did. The two of them have a whole secret history I know nothing about.

That means my best friend has been lying to me for ages! And I have no idea why.

MELODY

Not So Peaceful Melodies

Beethoven's Fifth sits on the music stand in front of me and it feels like a time bomb. As I stare at the bars and notes, panic butterflies rise up from my tummy and flutter around inside my throat. The strange shapes swim before me, becoming blurry and nonsensical.

I used to take piano lessons back when I was seven and I wanted to be just like Katie.

My parents were so happy that as soon as I told them they rushed out and bought me a glossy black grand piano—a Steinway & Sons, which is supposed to be the best, according to my dad, who did the research.

They went around telling people, "Kyle is the straight-A student and Melody is studying to be a classical pianist, which is fitting considering her name."

"Play me a melody," my dad would say on the rare evenings he was home. He'd laugh because he thought he'd come up with a superclever pun.

I tried, I really did. I wanted to be the Melody who made melodies. I wanted to sit down at the piano and close my eyes and make beautiful music, effortlessly. I struggled to read the notes on the page, yearned to understand them. I figured reading music would be like reading books, something I'd always loved. Except this was different. The piano bench was cold and hard and my feet didn't touch the ground. Sitting up straight with my wrists held high was a drag. Every time my fingers hit the keys it sounded awful, and whenever I practiced Kyle would cover his ears and complain. He'd tell our mom he couldn't focus on his homework because my playing sounded so awful.

I can't completely blame him. I did sound awful. But at least I tried. Not that my teacher believed me. Closing my eyes, I can still see Mr. Hurdy's chubby cheeks turning red and his blue eyes flashing with anger behind his horn-rimmed glasses. The dude had a mean streak. "What's the point of even coming, Melody, if you're not going to make an effort?" he'd ask. And what was I supposed to say? Truth was, I practiced for hours but I never got any better. Better for him to think I didn't try, because that was less embarrassing.

I came to dread the lessons so much I'd tear up from merely thinking about them. I begged my parents to let me quit and eventually they gave in, but they kept the piano.

"It doesn't matter that no one plays," my mom would say, sliding her hand along the shiny black surface. "It looks lovely in the living room."

It did.

But now I'm in a different living room. Katie's piano is brown and shabby and regular size, nothing grand about it, except for its origins. It belonged to her great-grandmother, who used to be a music teacher. The seat is more comfy than the one we have at my house. This is covered in a faded red corduroy cushion.

Jeff is saying, "I'm not hearing any music."

If only I'd stuck with the lessons a little longer, practiced more, learned the notes, or insisted on finding a teacher I wasn't afraid of.

But it's too late for wishful thinking. I've got to face the facts. I'm going to be discovered. Jeff and Anya will find out I'm an impostor and send me back home, regardless of who I look like, whose body I possess.

Before I sink my finger down on the key I hear someone pounding on the door.

I'm startled and the rest of the family is, too.

The knocking gets louder, angrier. I have a bad feeling about this.

Anya raises her eyebrows at Jeff, who gets up from the couch.

I jump up quickly, because I know who this must be.

"I'll get it," I say, rushing to the entryway. "I'm pretty sure it's for me."

As I open the door I stumble back. It's Katie in my body, and staring at her feels like looking at a mirror image of myself. Except not quite, because something is off. I am never this angry, yet the Melody in front of me is fuming—teeth gritted together, cheeks red, eyes narrowed. If there could be steam coming out of her ears right now, there would be.

"We need to talk," she hisses at me.

I'm shocked by not only her fury but also her wardrobe. She's wearing this tiny red dress that belongs to my mom with a pair of calf-length Ugg boots. Also, I can tell she broke into my mom's makeup. And in true Katie fashion she went way, way overboard: navy eyeliner, baby-blue eye shadow, a thick coat of mascara, bright-red lipstick, and even brighter blush.

"You look like a clown, Katie!"

"It's Melody to you," she says pointedly.

"Fine, Melody. Whatever. Do you realize you're revealing way too much cleavage? And the boots don't match that dress. Plus, why are you even wearing those boots in June? Aren't your feet hot?"

"Oh please," says Katie, running her hands through her hair. My hair, which looks stiff and shiny from all the gel she must've used. "Excuse me for finally putting some stylish clothes on your body."

"Everything okay?" Anya calls from the living room.

"Not now, Mom," Katie yells.

"Excuse me?" asks Anya.

I pinch her and whisper, "That's not your mom. She's mine!"

"Anya," she says. "I said, everything's great. I just need to talk to Katie for a few minutes."

"What about piano?" Anya asks.

"I'll practice after," I reply. "Promise!" Then I grab Katie's hand and pull her upstairs.

As soon as we are in my room, I close the door and turn on the stereo so no one can hear us.

"So, Kevin stopped by," Katie says.

Oh boy! Now I realize what the problem is.

"He did?" I ask. "That's strange." I look down at my feet because I can't meet her gaze.

"Don't play dumb with me!" she says.

Except she doesn't simply say the words—she growls them.

I could accuse Katie of plenty of things, too. Borrowing my stuff and never giving it back, always complaining about her family when they're so sweet and fun. But something in me makes it impossible. The arguments are swimming around in my brain but they never make it to my mouth. This always happens: I am too often left speechless. Dumbfounded. Which, it's no coincidence, has the word *dumb* in it.

I'm like this in school, too. Whenever I get called on in class, either an answer pops into my brain and I'm afraid it's the wrong one, or my mind goes blank. Then I think of the absolute perfect thing to say an hour later, when it's way too late.

"Don't just sit there!" Katie barks, standing over me.

I need to stall her. I need more time. "Why are you so upset, exactly?"

"You know why," Katie says. "Kevin kissed me. And why would Kevin kiss me, why would he even come over to my house, when we supposedly didn't even know each other? Except guess what, Melody? You do know Kevin. And obviously you have known him for a long, long time."

"Keep your voice down. They'll hear you," I whisper.

"Is that all you have to say?" she asks, shaking her head. "Not good enough. Kevin told me you two met in December, but you made him keep it a secret. Why would you do that?"

Katie is right to be upset. I lied and then I lied some more. This is just like our fight in August all over again, except worse. Maybe I should take this chance to really explain things, try to make her understand, except I don't even know where to begin.

She stomps her foot, impatient. "I'm waiting!"

I can't think faster than I'm already thinking. If I could, I would. I'm about to say something along these lines when my door bursts open and Ryan and Reese stumble in.

Katie, in my body, seems annoyed and she snaps at them, "Guys, we need privacy."

Reese and Ryan look up at her, shocked. Melody never talks to them like that. And it drives me crazy that she does. Not only is she making me look bad—she's being supermean to my favorite little guys.

I pinch her.

"Ouch!" she says, rubbing her arm. "That hurt!"

"Good, you deserved it. Don't snap at my brothers like that."

"Okay," she says, unhappily rubbing her arm. There's a red mark on her skin—on my skin. I wonder if it'll still be there when we switch bodies again. *If* we ever switch back.

"It's not okay—you need to apologize," I say.

"Sorry I yelled at your brothers," says Katie.

"No, not to me. You need to apologize to them."

Katie blinks and turns to the boys. "Sorry, Ryan.

Sorry, Reese. Katie is right. I should never yell at you guys."

She forces a smile and blinks hard. She's trying not to cry, I can tell.

Ryan grins back but Reese stares at her like he's trying to figure something out.

"You guys mind giving us some privacy? We're kind of in the middle of something," Katie says as she wipes a stray tear from her face.

"Who are you?" Reese asks Katie.

"What do you mean?" She sniffs. "I'm Melody."

Reese looks her up and down and says, "No, you're not. Your outfit is weird. You're not dressed anything like Melody."

Ryan nods, eyes wide. "And you're not acting like her, either. You're being mean like Katie."

"You think Katie is mean?" Katie asks, her hands on her hips. "Maybe she's had a hard time suddenly getting used to two little brothers who are in her face all the time. Maybe she needs some space because it's not always fun being outnumbered like that."

Well, now the boys seem even more suspicious. I shoot Katie a warning glance as I steer her brothers toward the door. "Guys, I love you but we need to talk right now. Okay? We can build a fort or play superheroes together later, I promise."

The boys leave, both of them looking over their shoulder, confused. I have the feeling they are on to us, which could be tricky.

Once we're alone and the door is shut and the music is turned up even louder, Katie is actually crying.

I sigh and sit down next to her on the bed and say, "I'm sorry, Katie. I didn't want to lie to you. I only did it because it seemed like it would be easier."

"He must think I'm horrible," she cries, wiping her eyes. She takes some deep breaths before continuing. "I'm so humiliated. Will you please tell me everything?"

There's no way out of this, so I decide to be honest with her. "Well, Kevin and I met over Christmas vacation when you were up in Seattle. He was visiting his dad, who's my neighbor. This is before Kevin decided to move to Braymar."

"Um, we did talk almost every single day, Melody. I think you might have mentioned meeting and falling in love with a gorgeous guy. Do our other friends know? Did you tell Ella and Bea?"

"No," I say, shaking my head. "I didn't tell anyone about Kevin and I didn't fall in love. We just hung out. And talked."

"And kissed," she adds.

"Not right away," I say with a sigh. "But eventually . . . yeah."

"I can't believe you had your first kiss and you didn't even tell me about it. Wait, Kevin was your first kiss, right?"

"Of course," I say.

"Well, how could you not think to tell your best friend? Or do you not consider me your best friend anymore? Why else would you keep kissing Kevin a secret? I mean, what is going on?"

I hate it when Katie gets pushy like this. Sometimes it's too much, her whole strong personality, how I end up seeming meek in comparison, when I'm not. Or at least, I don't want to be. "You don't get it. It's hard," I say.

"What's so hard about kissing an amazing guy? What's so hard about being beautiful and perfect and having everything? And fine, there's no law saying you had to tell me you met a cute boy over Christmas vacation. But it's so cruel to keep it a secret when you know how I feel about him. I mean I can't believe you let me call dibs on a guy you were already going out with!"

"That's my point," I start, but Katie interrupts me before I can finish.

"Is this what middle school is going to be like?" she asks. "You and Kevin off on your own, keeping major secrets from me?"

"This is not about you," I remind her.

"Of course it is!" she wails. "We're best friends—we

have been since forever. I tell you everything about my sad, pathetic life. And I thought you told me everything, too. But I was wrong—obviously. So why didn't you tell me?"

Something wells up inside of me. I can't keep quiet about this any longer. I'm sick of Katie's whole attitude. My best friend is resentful and completely wrong and I'm tired of it. So I take a deep breath and tell her, "Your life is not pathetic—it's awesome. And my life is far from perfect. Maybe I didn't tell you about me and Kevin because I'm sick of you saying things like that all the time."

Katie gasps, speechless for once in her life. But she recovers quickly.

"That is a rotten thing to say."

"Why? It's the truth," I say, standing up. "You asked how it's going to be in seventh grade? I don't know, but I'll tell you how it's not going to be. I'm not going to be sitting around waiting for you to tell me what to do. I have my own opinions and my own life. You're not allowed to decide you're in love with Kevin and no one else can have him. It's not fair. You can't call dibs on a boy, Katie, and you're not the boss of everyone."

"Don't call me Katie," Katie says, smugly. "You're Katie now. And I'm Melody."

I throw up my hands and say, "You're right. Hope you enjoy being me, Katie."

"Oh, I will," she says, turning around and heading out of my room.

I hear her stomp down the steps and then the door slams shut and then it's over—the screaming, the fighting, maybe our friendship, too.

KATIE

Nerds No More

I try too hard. I know I try too hard. I try too hard to meet boys and I try too hard in school and I try too hard in life. I reek of desperation, always have, but I can't help it.

Melody thinks I'm a big nerd and she's not the only one. I'm not in denial. I know I'm a big nerd. The thing is, we used to be nerds together. The two of us gawky and gangly, total geeks.

I don't know when things changed, exactly. It was subtle at first. People used to say we were both cute. Now everyone talks about Melody and how beautiful she is, how grown-up she's become. And me? No one says I'm beautiful. I don't mean to sound shallow. I know looks aren't everything. But they are certainly something. And it stinks having to watch everyone constantly fawning over your best friend while completely ignoring you.

It's like we've fallen into these roles. Melody gets to be mellow and gorgeous while I'm the high-strung witty sidekick. That's how everyone sees us. And I don't want to be the funny-looking best friend in middle school and beyond.

That's why things are so awesome now. Now I'm Melody through and through. I've got her looks and I've got her body and her boyfriend and her wardrobe and I am living in her fabulous house. I don't have to try too hard. I don't have to try, period. My life is perfect now and I, unlike the old Melody, will appreciate it. No, I won't just appreciate what she has—I'll enjoy it.

They say that living well is the best revenge, but that's not good enough. I'm going to show Melody how amazing life can be. I'll be a better Melody than Melody was herself. Starting right now.

Rather than head back to Melody's, I go straight to Kevin's place and knock on his front door.

His dad answers and says, "Hello, Melody. Nice to see you!"

"Um, sorry to stop by so late," I say. "Is Kevin home?"

"Sure thing. Why don't you come inside and I'll get him."

"Thanks." I step into the entryway and wait. I hope

my eyes aren't still glassy from the tears I shed earlier tonight. And if they are, I hope Kevin doesn't ask about them.

A minute later Kevin comes jogging down the steps. "Hey, Melo," he says. "What's up?"

"Hey. I know it's late but do you want to hang out?" I ask.

"Sure," he says, smiling his gorgeous smile. "How about we make s'mores?"

"Perfect!" I answer.

Moments later I'm in Kevin's backyard at his fire pit. We are roasting marshmallows. I've got four crammed onto my stick. He's just put on Beyoncé's latest and the moment could not be more perfect.

"I love summer," I tell Kevin, curling up next to him as I gaze into the dancing flames.

"Me, too," he says, shifting a little. "Hey, can I ask you a question? How come you've been acting so weird lately?"

"Lately like when?" I ask.

"Like at the beach," he says. "And earlier tonight. How come you took off so fast after I came to visit? And what's up with your outfit? Is that dress new?"

"It's my mom's," I tell him. "Isn't it awesome?"

"Are you wearing her makeup, too?" he asks.

"Yeah—do you like it?"

"I thought you didn't like makeup."

"I didn't." I shrug. "But I guess I changed my mind."

"Your hair feels weird," he says.

"I used some mousse and then some gel. And then more mousse. And hair spray so it wouldn't get messed up in case it got windy later," I explain.

"Hey, look out!" Kevin yells.

I sit up with a start and notice my marshmallows are on fire. I take them out of the flames and blow on them.

They are now charred and crispy, hard on the outside and kind of bitter. I take a bite out of one, anyway. "Yuck! This stinks," I say, tossing the marshmallow onto the ground.

Kevin is staring at me like he doesn't recognize me.

"What's wrong?" I ask.

"Nothing," he says. "Never mind."

MELODY

Color Me Blue

Anya knows it's been a rough night. Soon after Katie leaves she knocks on my door and asks if I want to talk about anything. I do, but I can't, obviously. She says I can have the night off from piano, which is a huge relief, but I still feel lousy.

I hate fighting—it's the worst. But maybe this had to happen. I've been annoyed with Katie a lot lately. And my entire summer has been spent wondering if we're even supposed to be best friends still.

Maybe we don't have enough in common anymore. Maybe we're simply drifting apart. Is this what happens when you grow up?

When we start seventh grade, we'll be at a different school on a brand-new campus. There'll be new kids, too.

Katie has been my best friend since before we could talk. But perhaps there's an expiration date on our friendship. Maybe we're like bananas that were left in the sun too long and spoiled.

Maybe it's time to move on.

I decide to go to bed early, and before I drift off to sleep this memory pops into my head from a bunch of years ago, back when Katie and I were seven.

We were at Color Me Lovely. The store had just opened up and we couldn't wait to go. Katie and I begged—literally begged—our parents on our hands and knees to take us there. They told us we had to wait for a special occasion. Except one day my mom had the flu, so my dad had the two of us on a Sunday, plus my brother, Kyle, whom he dropped off at a movie.

I think we were pestering him so much and he wanted to stare at his phone for a while longer that he finally agreed and dropped a hundred-dollar bill with the cashier and said, "Let these girls paint whatever they want. I'll be back in an hour." Then he was gone—much to our delight.

Katie and I held hands and giggled as we stared at the wall of options. They had everything: plates and bowls and cups; turtle planters; piggy, elephant, and goldfish banks. And figurines, too: mice, monkeys, dogs, and cats, hundreds of blank faces staring at us.

I paced back and forth in front of the shelves for a while, overwhelmed by the choices. Then my eyes rested on the perfect thing: a gigantic platter, smooth and flat and huge.

It was oval shaped, the biggest thing in the entire store, which seemed perfect because it'd leave me with endless space to create on. My mind was racing with possibilities and I couldn't wait to run over to the paint area to choose my palette, but of course I did wait because back then Katie and I did everything together.

When I took the platter off the shelf, it was so heavy that I almost dropped it. The woman working there said, "Are you sure you want this?"

I nodded, too excited to speak.

Katie was still looking at the wall of stuff and I didn't know why she was hesitating.

"Take a platter," I said. "It's okay, my dad already paid for it."

"No, let's start with something small," Katie said, pointing to a tiny little cup—the kind my parents drink espresso from.

I frowned, about to give in because I always did what Katie said, but that day was different. Something made me stop. I actually didn't want to paint a tiny mug. "That's no fun," I said, handing Katie my platter so I could climb the ladder and get another.

Katie didn't look happy, but she didn't complain, either.

We headed to the color station and the woman working there handed us a small plastic tray with space for six separate colors.

"I really need eight," I told her. She was wearing a paint-covered apron and seemed tired.

"Take twelve," she said, handing me a second palette. "There's only room for six colors in each one."

I squirted in my colors, starting with blue. Katie was right behind me and she did the same. I was glad I had two palettes because it turned out that twelve colors wasn't even that many. And in fact, it was hard to choose between cerulean blue and shimmery satin for my last square.

When I headed back to the table, Katie followed.

That's when I noticed she'd chosen every single color that I had, even the special blends and four shades of green, which surprised me. I'd passed on the red sparkle because there were only a few drops left and I wanted Katie to have it. Red sparkle was her favorite color back then. It still is. Except she didn't even choose it, she simply went and copied me twelve whole times.

I didn't bother pointing out her oversight because I didn't want her to feel bad.

I've always been worried about Katie feeling bad. Even at seven. That's when I started to notice her little comments. How she always wanted to be at my house even though we used to spend most of our time at hers. When I turned eight, I had a sleepover birthday party. Katie was there, of course, and so were Ella and Bea and a few other girls from school. As soon as we rolled out our sleeping bags Katie started in about how much bigger my room was than hers, and how my clothes were so much better, and she wouldn't stop. It was embarrassing, but I didn't know what to say, so I ignored her. And I kept ignoring her, even when those remarks increased.

It's like I blinked and suddenly it was too late. This is how she was with me and I couldn't stop her. It's how we were together.

But at Color Me Lovely none of that mattered. I was too busy thinking about the masterpiece I was going to create. I wanted busyness but clarity, distinct images but a lot of them. Like a page of computer icons except each one drawn by me—perfectly.

I found a tiny half pencil next to our station and I picked it up and started sketching a design on my plate. Before the graphite even hit the ceramic, Katie asked, "What are you doing? We're supposed to paint. Not draw."

If someone else were to talk to me like that, I'd think they were being way too bossy. But this was Katie's regular tone of voice.

"I'm going to sketch out my design first," I said, biting my bottom lip and staring at the heart I'd drawn, trying to decide if the sides were even. Making sure the two pillows are equally stuffed with the arches perfectly aligned is always the hardest part. I could've used a compass—that's what my brother would've done. But somehow that seemed wrong. I wanted to teach myself how to draw without it. I've always liked the look of free-hand better. It's so much more natural.

"Want to get a pretzel after this?" asked Katie. She was breathing down my neck, being annoying. I moved a few inches away from her.

"What's wrong?" she asked.

"Nothing," I said, feeling bad that she noticed.

Katie looked out the window. "And then I want to check out the new leggings at the Gap. Your silver pair are so cute, I think I should get the same ones. Or maybe I should get them in gold so we can be silver and gold together. Or maybe we should tell Ella and Bea to buy the gold pair and they can be the gold twins and we can be the silver twins and the four of us can be a whole shiny crew. Are you almost done?"

"We just got here," I reminded her. "And we've been wanting to paint something forever."

Katie rolled her eyes. "Not forever, Melo. Only since we saw the sign last month."

"It's been a few months," I said, and went back to my drawing, erasing one of the small clouds I'd made and redrawing it an inch to the left. Much better.

"So can we go?" asked Katie.

I cringed and lifted up my pencil, wanting to tell her to be quiet but not wanting to hurt her feelings. "Let's do this for a while," I said. "Okay?"

"Fine," Katie said, stretching out the word like she was annoyed at me for acting unreasonable.

She picked up a paintbrush and started painting right away, and I was impressed that she didn't want to draw out her idea first in erasable pencil. She's so much bolder than I am. I got lost in my own work. I drew tons of tiny little images: rainbows, hearts, stars, happy faces, a tree with a swing hanging off a high branch, a soccer ball, daisies and tulips, pink high-tops with rainbow laces, and little marshmallows bobbing in mugs of steaming hot chocolate—all the things I loved. I wanted to make a platter my family could look at and say, "That's so Melo."

I was halfway through, working on my second dog, this one a Dalmatian, when I noticed something out of the corner of my eye. Katie was standing up and stretching.

I glanced over at her platter, which she'd painted one shade of blue. "What are you going to do with it now?" I wondered.

Katie looked at me like I was crazy, like there was something wrong with me. "What do you mean, Melo? It's done."

I put down my own brush, stunned. "You're not

supposed to paint stuff a solid color, Katie. You're totally missing the point."

"The store is called Color Me Lovely and this is what I think is lovely," Katie said.

I stared at her platter. It was a pretty blue, yes, but it was so boring and uninspired. It looked like something you could buy at any store, not something a seven-year-old would go out of her way to create when given the freedom to make anything. "I know but isn't it kind of . . ."

"Kind of what?"

"Nothing," I said.

Katie looked over my shoulder. "Well, yours looks like some crazy cartoon!"

"Thanks," I replied, even though I could tell she wasn't exactly delivering a compliment. But crazy cartoons sounded cool to me.

That's the first hint I had that we were completely different people. Maybe I should've done something about it at the time, but instead we stayed besties for five more years.

It's funny to think about because at the moment, I can't even remember why.

The Kevin Situation

It's been days and Melody and I haven't spoken since our big fight and I feel bad, but also confused, like maybe I should apologize but I'm not sure what for, exactly.

I keep going over what happened, trying to figure it out, and I even wrote everything down in chronological order, like I'm studying for a test.

Day one of summer: Melody and I are sitting at the beach when a gorgeous guy walks by. "He's so hot," I say.

"You think?" Melody asks.

"I don't think, I know, and not only that—I'm in love."

Melody laughs. "You don't even know him."

"Doesn't matter. By the time this summer is over, I will. I'm totally calling dibs."

This would have been the perfect time for Melody to

say something like, "Oh, actually that guy is my neighbor and we're already going out." But Melody didn't say a
word. Why didn't she say anything to me?

July 4: It's a little before sunset. Melody and I are
camped out at McClaren Park, waiting for the fireworks
display. We've finished our picnic dinner and are playing
hacky sack. That's when I see Mystery Dude again. He
zooms by us on his skateboard before I can think of what
to say. Not wanting to miss another opportunity, I grab
the hacky sack and throw it at him. I hit the back of his
head and he stops, jumps off his board, and turns around,
surprised and maybe a tad annoyed.

"Sorry about that," I say, jogging over. "Guess I don't
know my own strength."

He looks at me and then at Melody and then at the
hacky sack I've scooped up off the ground. "Oh, no wor-
ries," he says.

"Hey, are you from around here?" I ask.

He smiles and tells me he's kind of new. He moved to
Braymar in June.

That was the beginning—or so I thought! I introduce
myself and Melody and the three of us watch the fireworks together, splayed out on my red-and-white-checked
picnic blanket.

July 6: I invite Kevin to hang out with us at the beach
and he shows up the very next day.

July 7 until that awful night in August: Melo and I hit the beach almost every single day and we see Kevin a lot. Sometimes he sits with us on the bus and sometimes he sits with his surfing buddies. He spends most of his time in the water but on occasion he'll come to land and play Frisbee with us. Once we split an order of cheese fries and twice he helps my stepbrothers build a tunnel. In all that time, Melody never tells me she likes Kevin. The two of them act like they hardly know each other.

August 15: I ask Melody to help me babysit for the twins. Melody tells me her mom won't let her come. Later that night my mom and Jeff decide to stay at home. I call Melody but she doesn't answer her phone. I decide to surprise her, except when I show up at her house, I'm the one who's surprised. That's when I find Melody and Kevin kissing in her hot tub.

And that was the beginning of the end of our friendship because Kevin was supposed to be mine.

Okay, maybe calling dibs on a guy shouldn't be allowed. It's quite possible that Melody wanted to tell me about Kevin, but I never gave her the chance. I have a strong personality. I know that. I've been accused of being bossy before, but never by Melody.

But I guess I shouldn't dwell on history. Not when everything is better now. Kevin is mine and we've been going to the beach every day, just the two of us.

Right now it's 8:45 and he's knocking on the door. I've raided Debbie's closet again and I know I look amazing, but I glance at myself in the mirror anyway before opening up the door. Gold bikini with sheer white sundress—check! Matching sun visor—check! Matching sandals—check! New gold-and-blue-striped bag—check!

When I open the door I find Kevin standing there with a gigantic chocolate donut.

"Here you go, Melo," he says, handing it over.

"Thanks." I smile and take a bite and chew and swallow. "Delicious."

"Wait, you've got a crumb on your lip," he says.

"I do?" I ask, wide-eyed.

"Yeah, let me get it for you," he says as he leans in and kisses me.

"Wow," I say, before I can stop myself.

Kevin laughs.

"I mean, um, cool. Is it gone?" I wipe my mouth, just in case.

"Is what gone?" he asks.

"The crumb," I say.

"Oh, I was just kidding about the crumb," he tells me.

"Oh yeah," I say, embarrassed now, blushing. "I know that. I was just kidding, too."

Wow, I am a dork. But now that I'm Melody my awkward behavior seems cute and Kevin doesn't hold it against me. He puts his arm around me and we walk to the bus stop.

We're turning the corner and are almost there when I spy something I don't want to see: a flash of red hair. Two flashes. It's Ryan and Reese. Melody is with them. I mean Melody in my body—Katie. They're playing with a balloon, trying to keep it aloft, laughing and giggling and having the best time.

I cannot face Melody now. There's no way! I think fast and throw myself to the ground. "Ouch," I yell.

"What's wrong?" asks Kevin.

"Um, I sprained my ankle. I need to go back to the house."

"Let's see," he says. "I am an EMT, remember?" He pulls his backpack off his back, unzips it, and starts rummaging around inside. "I should have an Ace bandage in here somewhere."

Uh-oh.

"Never mind," I say, standing up again. "I'm totally fine. In fact, I feel better already. That was a total false alarm."

Kevin looks from me to the bus stop and back again. "Is something going on?" he asks.

"No," I say. "I mean yes. I guess I don't feel like hitting the beach today. Let's do something else."

"What do you want to do?"

"Um, let's just hang out in my pool."

"But I'm supposed to meet Sanjay. We were gonna surf."

"You surfed yesterday and you can surf tomorrow," I say. "Please?"

"Okay, fine." Kevin shrugs and follows me back to the house. I put on my favorite radio station, get us some lemonade, and then put two rafts in the pool. Soon we are drifting.

"Isn't this so much better than the beach?" I ask.

"I don't know," says Kevin. He's wearing dark shades so I can't see his eyes, but he seems to be frowning.

"What's wrong?" I ask.

"Um, are you sure you hurt your ankle?" he asks.

I giggle out of nervousness. "Of course I did. I mean, it was a temporary thing and I'm completely better now. But why would I lie?"

"Maybe because you're avoiding Katie," he says.

I'm not sure of what to say, so I hop off and duck down underwater. Then I swim a few laps.

When I emerge from the water, Kevin is sitting on the edge of the pool with his legs dangling in. "I think you should come clean," he tells me. "Be honest with her. It's worse to pretend we're not a couple. She's going to find out the truth eventually and it's going to be bad."

"Hah!" I can't help but laugh because Kevin has no idea how messed up things already are.

"It's not funny," says Kevin. "She's your best friend. I know you're trying to spare her feelings and all, but it's not good."

I don't know what to say. Kevin is surprisingly perceptive and sensitive. It's totally annoying!

Another Day at the Beach

Katie is avoiding me. I know she is. I saw her and Kevin this morning when I was at the bus stop. The two of them fled as soon as they spotted us. I'm glad I was able to distract Ryan and Reese before they noticed her. They'd be crushed if they thought Melody didn't want to hang out with them and I don't want to put them through that kind of disappointment.

Sure, I'm a little upset that my best friend and my boyfriend won't speak to me, but I know things are pretty complicated. I need to focus on the positive. The sun is shining and the sky couldn't be a prettier shade of blue. Ryan and Reese look adorable in their coordinating, Hawaiian-print swimsuits. Reese is in blue. Ryan is in red. I'm having so much fun with Katie's brothers. It's like having life-size dolls to play with. Except with super-sweet and adorable personalities.

They're so excited to get to the beach. The two of them practically leap up the steps when the nine o'clock bus arrives. We are first on and they agree that we should sit in the front row, luckily. But then they fight over who gets the window seat.

"It's no fair. You got to sleep in the top bunk last night, so I should get the best seat on the bus," says Ryan.

"And you get the top bunk tonight," says Reese. "So I should get the window."

"Guys, why don't you take turns?" I say. "You can switch when we're halfway there."

"How will we even know that?" asks Ryan.

"The wishing tunnel marks the halfway point to the beach," I tell them.

"The what?" asks Reese.

"I mean the tunnel. You guys can switch when we get to the tunnel and then it'll be perfectly fair and square." I don't want them to know about the magic. They're too young. Who knows what they'd wish for: a lifetime sup-ply of cookie-dough ice cream, the freedom to watch tele-vision 24-7, or real live race cars? It's dangerous.

"Okay, fine," Reese grumbles. "But let me sit here first."

I agree, because he's already in the seat, and miracu-lously, Ryan does not complain.

We are on the bus and moving and the boys switch when we get to the tunnel and all is well.

When we get to the beach, we collect our things and scramble off the bus. We pick a spot by the lifeguard, because it seems like a smart thing to do.

"Last one in is a rotten egg," says Reese, racing to the water.

"No fair!" Ryan yells, following after him.

I slip out of my shorts and take off my shirt and join the boys.

Soon we're splashing in the surf, ankle-deep. The sand is cold and squishy and the water even colder. I am loving this. We race out and when the wave comes crashing down we run away screaming.

Later on we run into Amira and Jessie, two of my friends from school. They help us collect seaweed so we can decorate the castle we're building.

It's got five towers and a giant moat and a drawbridge made out of pebbles.

I'm coming back from the ocean with a bucket of water when Amira asks, "Where's Melody?"

It's not the craziest question. Melody and I spend most of our time together. But it still surprises me. I was having so much fun I'd forgotten about our fight and how she avoided me this morning at the bus stop. How she turned back and went home rather than actually speak to me.

"Don't know and don't care," I say.

Amira and Jessie both seem shocked.

Jessie asks, "Did you guys get in a fight or something?"

"Or something," I tell her. "It's complicated and I'd rather not talk about it."

KATIE

Lunch and Lunges,
but Not in That Order

On Saturday morning, I wake up to someone screaming Melody's name from downstairs. It's confusing until I realize she's calling for me.

"Melody? Melody, answer me!" Debbie is yelling with such intensity I'm kind of afraid to respond. Of course, I'm also afraid not to . . .

I hop out of bed and go to the railing.

"Yeah, Mom?" I ask, gazing down.

"Don't lean on the railing like that," she says. "It'll get loose again and I just paid Manny to tighten the screws."

"Sorry." I hold up my hands and back away.

Debbie makes her way upstairs. She's in workout clothes and her face is red and sweaty and she's guzzling water from a big bottle of Evian.

Whenever I see a plastic water bottle, the number thirty billion pops into my brain because that's how many plastic bottles end up in landfills every single year. It'll take a thousand years for all of those bottles to decompose.

That's not even the scariest thing about plastic bottles. They also contain a ton of gnarly chemicals and often those chemicals leach into the "purified" water they contain, which means the chemicals end up in your body and that can't be good.

A much safer option—as Jeff and my mom have been telling me for years—is to drink from a glass or stainless-steel water bottle, one you can clean and then refill with filtered water.

I'm surprised Debbie doesn't know this since she's all about healthy food and exercise. Yet there's nothing less healthy than ingesting a bunch of random chemicals. I don't say a word, though, because that's not Melody's style.

I won't say my best friend is meek because I'm not rude. But she's not one to stand up for herself or voice strong opinions. She'd rather stand back and let things happen around her.

Instead I wait patiently to see what Debbie has to say.

"Those thighs aren't going to stay that way if you don't work out," she warns.

I am not sure how to respond to this, so I keep my mouth shut. I do wonder why Debbie is worried about Melody's body, though. It's amazingly perfect.

"Come on. Let's do some lunges around the pool," Debbie says.

"I'm still waking up," I say, rubbing my eyes. This is both the truth and what I hope is a valid excuse.

"If you do lunges with me now we can go shopping afterward," Debbie says, grinning.

Suddenly I'm wide-awake. My mom hardly ever takes me shopping and when she does she's all about Old Navy and Target and wherever is having a big sale.

Something tells me *sale* isn't a part of Debbie's vocabulary. It doesn't need to be.

A Saturday afternoon shopping spree sounds amazing. I stretch my arms up over my head and grin. "Okay, I'll do it! Just give me a few minutes to change."

"See you downstairs in five," says Debbie, pointing to her big gold watch. "I will be timing you."

Once she's gone, I head to the bathroom and splash cold water on my face. Then I slip out of my pajamas and into a pair of black spandex capris and a blue tank top, pulling my curls into a tight ponytail on top of my head.

Melody's mom is doing sit-ups when I get downstairs. She's out of breath but still moving fast.

I stand there and wait for her to finish.

"Come on, lazy bones. Join me!" she huffs.

"I said I'd do lunges," I reminded her. "Not sit-ups."

"When I said *lunges* I meant work out with me. Come on, babe. Didn't you say you had nachos on Monday? And I can tell you've been roasting marshmallows again. Your hair smells like smoke."

I quickly grab a lock of my hair and sniff. She's right. It smells like last night's bonfire with Kevin. We've been roasting marshmallows almost every night this week. And spending our days at the beach, which has been incredible.

It's funny, though. I'd forgotten about the nachos from Monday. I wonder why Debbie cares. I mean, what's the big deal? So I had lunch. Everyone has lunch. But before I defend myself, I think, what would the real Melody say in this situation? And the answer is nothing.

We do sit-ups and then lunges around the pool. Our hands are on our hips and we are bobbing in time.

"It's like we're soldiers in the war against fat," Debbie says.

I laugh because this is genuinely funny. When I think about wars, images of backyard swimming pools surrounded by white and lavender roses don't really come to mind.

Except Debbie seems totally serious.

We lunge until I'm out of breath. "How much longer?" I huff.

Debbie checks her watch. I didn't realize she was timing us. "Another minute and then we can move on to free weights."

"I never agreed to free weights," I argue, forgetting for a moment to act more like the real Melody. This is getting hard and it's hot out.

"Humor me, Melo. Pretend this is fun."

The swimming pool is gorgeous, but after a while the scenery gets boring.

"Hey, why don't we go to the beach?" I ask.

Debbie's nose crinkles up. "Too sandy. Plus, you and Katie have been there every day this week. That's why I got you the bus pass."

I gulp, guiltily.

"We could hike," I suggest.

I realize that today is Saturday, which is my real family's hiking day. Okay, it's a drag getting up early in the morning, but hiking an actual mountain is way more fun and probably better exercise than endless lunging around the swimming pool.

"Too dusty," Debbie replies.

I am out of ideas. I wonder if Melody does this a lot. Exercises with her mom, I mean. If so, she never told me.

Twenty minutes later, after the lunges and the weights

and the leg lifts, I am panting and exhausted and ready to lie by the pool.

"Let's go in," says Debbie, waving a hand toward the water.

"Great idea!" I say. "I could float around for an hour, at least."

"Are you kidding, lazy bones? We're doing laps!"

"No," I groan. "My arms feel like they're going to fall off."

"You'll be fine," says Debbie. "And you do want to go shopping after this, correct?"

She's got me there. We go in to change into bathing suits and when we get back, we each do ten laps freestyle and ten of the breaststroke and then three butterfly and then, when I feel as if I can't move, I tell her I'm done.

"Great. We already worked off our lunch. We're way ahead of the game."

"So we can actually shop now?" I ask.

Debbie smiles as she readjusts her ponytail. "Sure. Meet me at the car in twenty."

She hops out of the pool, grabs a towel, and heads inside.

Soon we're in Debbie's car zooming toward the mall and then we are inside, where Muzak pumps in from invisible speakers, real plants look plastic, and everything is bright and shiny.

Our first stop is a boutique where every salesperson knows Debbie and Melody by name. Debbie immediately finds a slinky silver cocktail dress for herself. "This will be perfect for the Fourth of July," she says, admiring the dress on the hanger.

"Where are we going?" I ask.

"Oh, we're not going anywhere. But your father and I are going to be in San Francisco," she says. "At least that's what he promised. He'll probably find some excuse and back out of it, last minute. You know your father . . ."

I don't, actually, so again I stay silent.

Debbie doesn't notice. She tries on three more dresses that would be perfect for the event but she can't make up her mind, so she buys them all.

Our next stop is the juniors department at Nordstrom. I try on a pair of skinny jeans and a silky white tank top. On Katie it would look ridiculous, I'm sure. But on Melody, it's gorgeous. I look sixteen and stunning and I cannot stop looking at myself in the mirror. I am pleased, to say the least. And Debbie is, too.

"I used to be young and thin like you," she says with a sigh. She keeps making weird comments like this, but whatever. We buy the jeans and the top and two dresses. One is red and the other is black with a gold shiny stripe running down the side. Both are short and kind of tight.

Not exactly Melody's style, but they look so amazing, I can't pass them up.

Next I pick out a zebra-striped dress and hold it up to my body, admiring myself in the mirror. "Animal prints?" asks Debbie, raising her eyebrows.

"Is it too much?" I ask, checking the price tag and trying not to look too shocked by the number printed on it. I have never spent even close to this amount of money on an item of clothing and I don't think my mom has, either.

"No, I'm just surprised. But go ahead and try it on. I'm sure it'll look stunning on you."

I try the dress on. It does look amazing—clingy in all the right places. We buy the dress and some matching wedge sandals and a new headband and silver hoop earrings to go along with it.

Then we get three more pairs of designer jeans each, the kind my mom always says are a waste of money.

When all the new clothes are piled up on the counter by the cash register, they tower over me and Debbie and the saleslady.

I'm wondering if Debbie's going to ask me to cut it in half or take out a few of the pricier things, except she isn't even paying attention. She's on her cell making an appointment with her hairdresser.

When the saleslady adds everything up and gives us the number, Debbie throws down her credit card without even blinking. I don't even know if she heard the final amount but she doesn't seem concerned, either way.

She only seems annoyed that we have to stand around for another five minutes while the saleslady folds everything and wraps it in tissue paper and tucks it into bags.

Now that Debbie is off the phone she rolls her eyes at me, impatient.

Once the bags are ready, I grab them—three of them stuffed full—and we head to the shoe department. Same deal—everything I want I get. New pink Uggs, flip-flops with sparkly rhinestones, black strappy leather sandals and the same pair in brown because I can't decide between the colors. "Get both," says Debbie, looking bored.

"Ready to go to lunch?" she asks as the guy in the shoe department is running her card.

I nod. "Sure."

Rather than go to the regular old food court, we find a table at the fancy café at the other side of the mall.

Debbie gets a salad with light Italian dressing on the side. When I try to order my favorite—an eggplant pizza with extra cheese—Debbie puts her hand on my arm and says, "Sweetie. Do you really need extra cheese? Do you know how much cheese goes into a regular pizza?"

I shrink back from her. "Yeah, not enough," I say. "That's why I ordered extra."

"Well, I hope these cute new clothes still fit you after this meal," she jokes. At least I think she's joking. She lets me go ahead with my order, but doesn't look too pleased.

Soon after that her phone pings with a text. She reads it and then says a bad word I won't repeat.

"What's wrong?" I ask.

"Your father promised me he'd be back tonight, but now he's stuck in San Francisco with another work crisis. We're supposed to have dinner with the Demseys at Raul's and you know it's impossible to get a table at Raul's. I've been waiting to go there for months. But does your father care? No!"

"You can still go without him," I say.

My mom smiles to herself, sadly. "It wouldn't be the same."

Melody told me her mom gets Botox treatments that take away any expression on her face, but it's not true. Debbie's forehead doesn't wrinkle like a normal person's, but she still looks sad.

"Want to see a movie? Maybe we can invite Anya and Katie over," I say before I can stop myself. My mom and Debbie never hang out anymore and they probably haven't spoken in years. It's an absurd suggestion. But I don't know, I guess I'm missing my real mom. Even though it hasn't been that long.

"I don't think Anya is interested in hanging out with me. No offense, sweetie. She's got better things to do."

When the check comes Debbie doesn't even glance at it. She just plucks her AmEx out of her wallet and places it on top of the little folder.

"Ready?" she asks, picking up her shopping bags.

I grab mine, too. When we get to the car, Debbie's mom opens her trunk.

We throw the bags inside. I didn't think there was such a thing as too much shopping but I am exhausted down to my bones.

When I head to the passenger side of the car and open the door, Debbie asks, "Where are you going? You only want to do one round today?"

I laugh because I think she's kidding. It seems like we bought out half the mall. Except no. Debbie is totally serious!

MELODY

Wrong Order

I'm in the middle of some crazy dream when I hear pounding on my door. It's a hard, heavy sound that I don't register at first, probably because I'm not expecting it. I open one eye and look at the clock, which reads 6:00 a.m. Who could be at my door at that crazy hour? And wait a second! Who am I?

I check my arm. It is still skinny and freckled, which means I'm still in Katie's body. Phew! I've had the most amazing week, hanging out with her brothers. We've been to the beach every single day and it's been awesome. We've splashed in the surf and made sand castles and I even struck a deal with Anya. As long as I take care of Ryan and Reese, I don't need to practice piano. It's a total win-win situation. Except I assumed I'd get the weekends off.

"Wait, I'm coming," I mumble, but the door opens before I manage to get out of bed.

I rub my eyes and sit up. Things are foggy at first but soon Reese and Ryan come into focus.

The boys are dressed in matching green sweatpants and white T-shirts with mysterious unmatching stains in various places. They are ready for the day, which makes no sense. Because last time I checked, it was Saturday.

"Time to hike!" Reese tells me.

I roll over and bury my head in the pillow. "Too early!" I say with a groan, except of course my words come out muffled.

The boys race out of the room and I drift back to sleep, despite their noise.

A few moments later, someone knocks on the door again. This time it's Anya. "Katie, sweetie. It's time for our family hike. Let's go!"

"Hold on," I call, rubbing my eyes.

I glance at the clock again, thinking I must've read it upside down. It's got to be nine o'clock, right? No, the clock will only stand up this one way. But what is Anya talking about? Is she kidding?

Katie's whole family is standing in the doorway staring at me as if I am some creature in a cage. A perplexed and kind of lazy creature. This isn't a joke.

I sit up fast. "Sorry, everyone. I'll get ready."

"Okay. Glad you are finally up. We'll give you privacy while you change," says Anya. "See you downstairs in five."

She shuffles the boys out of the room and I swing my feet around onto the floor. Hiking. An early morning hike. Is six o'clock even morning? It feels like the night before. How am I supposed to hike?

Well, I'm not sure but I suppose it'll help to dress the part. I try to open up one of Katie's dresser drawers, but it's jammed so tightly with clothes, it won't budge. I try the closet next. Not only do the doors swing open, everything comes tumbling out. Ugh. She's such a slob! I can't even tell what's clean and what's dirty. What I can tell is that everything is kind of wrinkled. I grab a pair of white shorts and a blue T-shirt. Actually, it's my blue T-shirt. I lent it to Katie months ago and forgot all about it. It's as soft as butter, the kind of shirt that looks great on everyone. It's also nicer than any other shirt in Katie's wardrobe. No wonder she borrowed it.

I pull on socks and lace up Katie's hiking boots. They are hot pink, which is weird—yet another example of Katie's bold and misguided attempts at fashion. Hiking boots should be brown or tan—the color of dust. That's what they'll end up looking like, anyway. But there's no one to explain this to and no other shoes for me to wear.

Ten minutes later we climb into the station wagon. I

end up smushed between Ryan and Reese's car seats. It's a good thing Katie's so skinny. There's barely room to breathe, which is okay, actually. Because when I do breathe in, I smell peanut butter and jam.

I don't know why Katie's parents don't get a bigger car—a Tesla with a third row, maybe, or even a minivan. Maybe I'll suggest that later on. Because it doesn't seem fair, making Katie ride everywhere squished in the middle.

When we finally get to the trailhead it's six thirty and the sun is barely peeking out over the mountain.

Ryan and Reese race ahead as soon as they are out of the car. "Wait for everyone else," Jeff calls, running after the boys, who scramble away with pretend squeals of fear. He roars like a lion and scoops them both up at the same time, one in each arm. They giggle with delight.

Once he puts the boys down again, they're off, kicking up dust with their heels, racing and tripping up the mountain like only Ryan and Reese can.

Katie's mom is watching, eyes sparkling. She links her arm in mine and we march behind them. I'm still waking up, yawning and rubbing my eyes and missing Katie's cozy bed. Still, this isn't so bad. The sun has just risen and it's not yet warmed the canyon. It's chilly, but the cool feels nice. I zip up my hoodie and pull it over my chin so the fuzzy inside rubs against my skin.

The mountain is steep and the guys are ahead of us. Ryan and Reese keep stopping to pick up stones and twigs. They throw pebbles into the canyon below and, at one point, try to drag a branch the size of the two of them put together.

Jeff and Anya laugh at their efforts and I watch it all, amazed. This is so superfun. Katie used to complain to me about family hikes. Waking up before the sun, being forced to spend time with the boys . . . She always tried to sleep at my house on Friday nights so she could skip the outing. Like I said, she doesn't appreciate her perfect life. She's the luckiest girl I know.

Once I'm actually awake and able to enjoy it, the hiking is awesome.

We zigzag up the switchbacks for close to an hour, getting higher and higher. The fresh air feels awesome and crisp. My legs ache but in a good way. There are birds and lizards and wildflowers growing out of cracks in the mountain. When the boys finally start to complain that their feet are tired, we turn around and head down.

My stomach is growling, so I'm thrilled when Jeff suggests stopping for breakfast at Jinkey's Café. I love Jinkey's and my mom won't ever take me. She's wary of any popular breakfast place. Plus, Jinkey's has refused to cook her egg-white omelets without butter or oil.

We squeeze into a booth: Jeff and Anya on one side

and the boys and me across from them. I make snakes out of the boys' straw wrappers, drip water on them, and watch them grow. Ryan and Reese shriek in delight like they've never seen this trick before.

"You're the best big sister, Katie," Reese says.

"Thanks, buddy."

"I have to pee," Ryan says, squirming in his seat. "Katie, will you take me?"

"Of course," I reply, standing up and helping Ryan out of the booth.

I notice Jeff raise his eyebrows at Anya, both of them surprised. I should argue, I guess. Tell him I'm too busy, but I don't have the heart.

"Let's go, little dude."

When I put my arm around Ryan, he beams up at me and it warms my insides.

When we get to the bathroom, Ryan says, "I don't actually need help but I don't like to go by myself."

"That's cool, buddy," I say. "I felt the same way when I was your age."

By the time we get back to the table the waitress is there and ready to take our order.

"Chocolate-chip pancakes," Reese declares loud enough for the entire restaurant to hear.

"Me, too," says Ryan.

Jeff gets eggs and toast and Katie's mom asks for a

vegetable frittata and a corn muffin. A corn muffin sounds divine and I order one, too. Plus eggs and bacon, which is my big mistake.

"What did you say?" asks Anya.

I look up, alarmed, thinking Anya must be worried about fat. My mom has talked to me about nutrition and wasted calories enough that I know I'm supposed to order egg-white omelets and at least two vegetables: spinach, tomatoes, mushrooms, or peppers—something to make it healthy. But I didn't think Jeff and Anya would care about that stuff. They included plenty of simple carbs in their orders. So what's wrong with mine? Why are they staring at me like I've grown six heads?

Suddenly I realize the problem: the bacon.

I ordered bacon and Katie's a vegetarian!

KATIE

Typical Saturday

Debbie is watching me as I stare at the trunk of her car, now stuffed full of bags. The realization dawns on me slowly. "We're dropping these off so we can do more shopping?" I ask.

"Of course," says Debbie. "I'm sure there's more damage we can do."

We head back to the mall and we pick up some new swimsuits and after that I can't even remember what else I bought.

Three hours later, we're getting pedicures in the living room. Debbie's people come to her. I have my feet up and am reading *People* magazine. One of my favorite singers was arrested for drag racing without a license. Another checked herself out of rehab and shaved her head. It seems weird. If you're supersuccessful and rich and everything, why can't you just kick back and enjoy life? Maybe go on vacation or go to a spa or take a trip to Australia or somewhere else cool?

I don't understand, but I do understand what too much shopping is. I am exhausted and my feet ache. Melody's mom is tired, too. She's complaining about a callus on the bottom of her foot and her manicurist, Daisy, assures her she'll shave it off. This sounds gross, so I bury my head in the magazine again.

Soon there's a knock on the front door.

"Can you get that, Daisy?" Debbie asks.

Daisy opens the door and in walks some dude with a giant massage table and some fluffy-looking towels.

"You're early," says Debbie.

"You have a masseuse come to you?" I ask.

Debbie looks at me, surprised.

"I mean of course you have the masseuse come to you." I cough. "I knew that. Um, what's the occasion?"

Debbie is still staring—her skinny eyebrows raised high.

"There is no occasion, Melody. You know that. This is just a typical Saturday."

Later that night I'm alone in Melody's room with nothing to do. Kevin went to the Dodgers game with his dad. Ella and Bea are at sleepaway camp in Wisconsin for the entire summer. Jenna is with her grandparents in Mexico this month and Melody is probably babysitting for Ryan and Reese. I wish I could call her, except I know I'm the last person she wants to hear from.

And while it seems like I want to call because I'm bored and there's no one else to hang out with, that's not totally true.

I actually want to call Melody because I miss her.

MELODY

Supertwins

"I'm just kidding about the bacon," I blurt out, practically in tears. The waiter is still watching me, pen poised, with no idea of the stakes. "I meant veggie bacon. You have that, right?"

I don't know what veggie bacon is. If it exists, even. But veggie hot dogs exist and veggie burgers do, too. I've seen Katie order them. So why not veggie bacon?

It's my best way out of this. Katie's whole family is staring at me like I'm some foreign being possessing her body, which I suppose I am.

Not that her parents have any actual clue.

I hope they don't have a clue.

I don't know what would happen if I were discovered. Like, what if Ryan and Reese shared their suspicions and

Anya and Jeff took them seriously? It wouldn't be hard to figure out the truth. Just sit me down in front of a piano and force me to play. Or ask me to do complex fractions or how to spell *suffragette*. I'm totally bad at stuff like that and a lot more. Katie is a brain and I am not. If Anya and Jeff figured out the truth, I'd probably have to switch back. But would it happen automatically? Or would Melody and I have to go through the wishing tunnel again? Or maybe they'd tell my mom and make me go home, regardless of whose body I was in. I'm so not ready for any of that.

"I don't think we have any veggie bacon," the waiter tells me. He says *veggie bacon* like it's in another language, like he's never heard of it before.

"No problem," I say with a smile as I hand back the menu and ignore the stares. "Had to check. I'll stick with the eggs and corn muffin. Oh, and I'll take a hot chocolate, too. With marshmallows."

Uh-oh. I ordered marshmallows out of habit but I should've skipped them because Katie doesn't really eat them. Reese glances at me for a moment, like he's trying to figure something out, but he doesn't say a word and no one else seems to notice.

Everything is back to normal. Our food arrives and we have breakfast. I go for the hot chocolate right away and the funny thing is, the marshmallow doesn't taste as delicious as usual. Before I have a chance to ponder the meaning of this I hear the twins fighting. Reese thinks Ryan has bigger pancakes and Ryan is sure that Reese's portion has more chocolate chips.

"I can settle this," Jeff says. He takes both plates and switches them.

Magically, this appeases the boys. They dig in. I do, too. Everything tastes amazing and it's awesome being able to eat without my mom staring at me, counting calories in her head and disapproving of the way I chew. She's probably doing that to Katie right now, and I cringe at the thought. Of course, maybe it'll be good for Katie to see how imperfect my life actually is.

After breakfast, Ryan and Reese race to the car and Reese starts crying because Ryan gets there first. "He cheated." Reese pouts.

"Did not," says Ryan.

"Did too," Reese insists.

Ryan yells, "Did not did not did not."

"Did too." Reese stamps his foot.

"Did too," Ryan says with a grin.

"Did not," Reese replies, and then pauses, confused.

Ryan claps his hands and dances around in triumph. "Hah! Exactly. I did not cheat. You said so yourself." It's a dirty trick. I know because Kyle used to trip me up like that when we were kids.

I put my arm around Reese and whisper in his ear, "I'll bet you'll beat him next time."

Reese sniffs and wipes his nose with the back of his hand and climbs into the car, letting me help strap him into his car seat.

Everyone's quiet until we get home and then the twins start fighting over their race cars.

I never realized how competitive the boys are. I try to reason with them but quickly learn there is no reasoning with four-year-olds. They are irrational.

I need a break, so I head upstairs to hide in Katie's room. Except it's not exactly relaxing being here because it's such a mess. I don't know how she lives this way, and I realize I don't have to know. I'll change things up and organize it myself.

First, I take everything out of her closet, and then I tackle the dresser drawer. Both are a mess of sweaters tangled up with leggings and inside-out T-shirts and jeans that haven't fit her since we were in the fourth grade. It takes me an hour to sort and separate. By the time I finish, I find three more of my T-shirts, two pairs of my jeans, my argyle socks, and an ankle bracelet my parents got me when they went to Paris last year. Also, a stuffed animal I left at a sleepover at Katie's house when we were nine.

I can't get mad because I know Katie's not keeping my

stuff on purpose. She's simply that unorganized. Anyway, by the time I'm finished, there's a system that makes sense. All of Katie's jeans are together, and I've also grouped her dresses, skirts, and shirts. Sweaters are folded and in a drawer and there's a giant bag of stuff that's stained or way out of style or doesn't fit her anymore or is way too ugly to wear.

Once I'm done, I'm feeling much better. I can finally relax, except I can't because the twins have burst into the room.

They don't believe in knocking. It's pretty cute. Usually.

"Wanna play superheroes with us?" Reese asks. He's holding a throw pillow from their living room couch.

"Okay, can I be Superman?" I ask.

"I'm Superman," says Ryan, chest out proud.

"What about Batman?" I ask.

Reese shakes his head. "No, that's taken, too."

I wrack my brain trying to come up with another superhero name but can't.

"Who should I be?" I ask.

"Catwoman or Wonder Woman," says Ryan, like it's obvious.

"Those are my only two choices?" I ask, putting my hands on my hips. "What if I want to be the Hulk?"

"You're a girl. You can't be the Hulk," Reese says, giggling.

"It's make-believe," I insist. "I can be whoever I want to be."

The boys don't know how true that statement is, and I laugh to myself. I'm having fun. And just as I suspected, it's so much better to be the older sibling than the younger. The boys look up to me and it feels great. I call the shots but I'm not going to be a jerk about it. I'm not going to be anything like my real big brother, Kyle.

I pull a green sweatshirt out of Katie's dresser drawer and throw it on. "I'm the Hulk. GGGGRRRR!!!"

Then I chase the boys through the house out to the backyard. Being Katie is awesome. She doesn't know how great she has things!

KATIE

Surfer Dude

I have been Melody for almost two weeks now and it keeps getting better. I shop. I get to watch as much TV as I want to. When Debbie is out I get to sleep in. Mornings she's home it's workout central but that's okay. After we're done exercising, I get to lie around and watch TV or hang out at the beach with Kevin. My boyfriend.

We ride the beach bus together almost every day and it's amazing. In fact, that's where we are right now. Kevin is taking a nap and I am right next to him. I can hear him breathe. Actually, I can hear him snore. This happened yesterday and the day before that, too. Okay, who am I kidding? This happens every single day.

I used to think that everything Kevin did was cute. Guess what? The snoring is the exception.

That's okay, though. I don't blame him for needing sleep. We did wake up extra early so we could take the first bus of the day, which leaves at seven. Kevin is the one who insisted we get to the beach this early. Apparently that's when the best waves roll in. And I'm not going to complain because taking the earliest bus means we avoid Melody and Ryan and Reese.

Kevin is smart to sleep on the ride here. I wouldn't mind napping, either. Except it's impossible for me to relax with him leaning on my shoulder, which, I just realized, is feeling a little damp.

It must be sweat, is what I'm thinking. Except it's kind of cool out this morning.

It can't be drool, can it?

Oh no, that would be too icky. There's no way.

Except I smell cherry-flavored ChapStick, which can mean only one thing . . .

I carefully turn my head, look down, and wish I hadn't.

Kevin is drooling on my shoulder.

Yeah, drooling.

It's nice that he feels comfortable enough to do this.

That's what I tell myself, anyway. And to be fair, there was a time when I thought that anything Kevin did was amazing—even when he drooled. Except that time is not now.

At least the bus is finally pulling into the parking lot. I shake Kevin awake.

"We're at the beach!" I say.

"Leave me alone, Mom," he says, crankily.

I laugh. "Um, Kevin? It's me, Melody. Not your mom. You're on the bus. Remember?"

"Huh?" He sits up with a start and blinks a few times. "Oh yeah. I wasn't snoring, was I?"

"No," I lie.

"Good." Kevin coughs. "Actually I don't know why I even asked you that because I don't snore."

"Of course you don't," I say.

He smiles at me and runs his hands through his hair to try to straighten out his bed head. It doesn't work. Then he reapplies his ChapStick. The cherry-flavored smell was getting to me, so last week I took his ChapStick out of his bag while he was surfing and threw it in the trash. But he must have a supply at home because it's back.

His surfboard is stored underneath the bus. After we get off, we wait in silence for the driver to unlock the compartment and unload.

As soon as Kevin grabs his board he heads toward the water, not waiting for me and not looking over his shoulder to see if I'm following, although of course I am. The sky is overcast because apparently it's even too early for the sun. I point this out to Kevin, but he doesn't laugh. He's not paying any attention to me.

"Yo, check it out!" says Kevin, gazing at the ocean. He

may be a snoring drooler but he was right about the waves. They are huge.

We find a spot near the surf. After I spread my towel on the sand, I peel off my blue sundress to reveal a matching blue bikini. It's just one of the new outfits I picked up on my latest shopping spree with Debbie. I expect a reaction because I know I look amazing, but Kevin is too busy putting on his wet suit to notice.

After he zips up the back, he picks up his surfboard, tucks it under his arm, and is about to head to the water when I stop him.

"Wait. Can you help me with my sunscreen?" I ask, waving the bottle in front of his face.

"Sorry, I've gotta go," he says, pointing to the water. "This surf is too gnarly. I can't wait another second."

I figure he's joking, because what kind of boyfriend says he doesn't have time to help his girlfriend apply sunscreen? Except he's not kidding. Kevin is that kind of boyfriend.

Stunned, I watch him jog into the white water and beyond. He paddles his way out and soon he is lost among the throng of surfers straddling their boards and bobbing up and down in the waves.

Last week I was okay with this. It was enough to know I was at the beach with my boyfriend. It didn't matter that once we got there he pretty much ignored me. Now, though, the fact that we don't actually hang out at the beach together is kind of annoying.

I do my best to apply sunscreen by myself. Then I rifle through my tote bag and pull out my Debbie-approved snack. It's a gluten-free almond butter, chia seed, and spinach ball and let me tell you, it tastes about as appealing as it sounds. Meaning, not so much. After one tiny nibble I walk over to the nearest trash can and throw it away.

That's when I notice the snack stand is opening up. They're already cooking French fries, the smell of which makes my stomach rumble with hunger.

Last night's dinner was raw sprouted veggie burgers. Afterward, I convinced Debbie to take me to the new sorbet place on the corner, but once we got there she made me order a single scoop even though I really wanted a triple.

Thinking about this depresses me. Sighing, I head back to my towel and flop down, exhausted, hungry, and bored. I check my watch, amazed that I've only been here for fifteen minutes. The beach used to be my favorite place in the world. Summertime always felt magical. Except now that the magic has actually happened? Well, it's kind of disappointing.

I miss hanging out at the beach with the real Melody. I wonder what she's doing today. She's probably just waking up, maybe making a Lego city with the twins or playing superheroes or building a fort out of couch cushions. Of course, none of that sounds so bad right about now.

Closing my eyes, I decide to take a nap.

When I wake up the sun is blazing high across the sky. Squinting out at the waves, I still see about a dozen surfers. Kevin is probably among them. His green backpack is still here next to me, anyway, so I know he hasn't gone home.

I stand up and stretch and take a walk because there is nothing else to do.

I've only gone a few yards when I hear someone whistle. I turn around, but can't tell where it came from, which is so creepy! I'm only in the bikini and I wish I'd worn the cover-up. I should know better by now. In Melody's body I get all sorts of attention. It's funny how I used to crave it. Now, I'd kind of like to hide. I'm thinking about this when I hear some familiar voices. It's Ryan and Reese.

They're building a sand castle with Melody.

"We need more seaweed for the curtains," Melody is telling them.

This makes me smile. Melody always insisted on hanging curtains in our sand castles and it's good to know that some things never change, even though we are now grown-up. And in each other's bodies.

I wonder if I should say hi. They seem pretty happy

without me. And I don't want things to get awkward. Because technically we're still fighting, even though I don't really want to be. Melody is probably still furious and I totally don't blame her.

I'm backing up, about to turn away, but before I do so, Ryan sees me and runs over. "Melody!" he yells, jumping into my arms with so much force I stumble back.

Once I regain my balance I squeeze him tight. I've missed the smell of his shampoo and his squirmy little body. So much so that tears form in my eyes.

"Where've you been?" he asks. "We haven't seen you all summer."

I'm not sure what to say. It's way too complicated. I set him down and then Reese leaps into my arms, not to be outdone.

I giggle and say, "I've missed you guys so much. What are you doing?"

"We're building a fortress for cars and boats and planes," says Reese.

"With curtains, because Katie says we need them," Ryan adds.

"That makes sense," I say with a nod.

Melody is focused on building, not looking at me. She's wearing a shirt that's not mine and at first I wonder if she convinced my mom to take her shopping—although that never happens. Then I realize the T-shirt is hers. I borrowed it and then lost it but I suppose she unearthed it. Knowing Melody she probably cleaned out my whole closet.

I was already feeling like a lousy friend and seeing her recovered T-shirt just makes things worse. I am the worst!

"Are you still acting mean like Katie?" Reese asks, staring into my eyes with a serious expression on his face.

"Katie is acting nice now," Ryan says to Reese.

"I know that," says Reese. "I mean the old Katie."

"You guys are crazy," I say, ruffling Reese's hair. "No one is mean and there is no old Katie."

I peek at Melody. She's looking at me out of the corner of her eye, I can tell. I miss my best friend. My old best friend, I should say. Are we still best friends? If not, will we ever be again? I hope so.

"How's everything going?" I ask.

"Good," she says, carefully. "You?"

"Great," I say, lying. "I'm here with Kevin."

I don't know why I blurt this out and now I feel awkward, but Melody doesn't seem to mind. She shrugs and says, "Yeah, I figured."

I wave toward the ocean and say, "He's surfing."

She nods. "Um, no big shocker there."

We share a smile. So much is left unsaid. I want to hang with my stepbrothers. Should I ask? Is that weird? This whole thing is weird.

"I miss you!" I blurt out.

"Me, too," says Melody as relief floods her face. "Um, sorry about everything. I should've told you the truth a while ago. And I shouldn't have snuck around."

"I'm sorry, too. I shouldn't have called dibs on Kevin. That's not fair. I didn't even know him. I probably never gave you the chance to tell me the truth."

"Um, what are you guys talking about?" asks Reese.

"Nothing," I tell him.

"Hey," says Melody, standing up and brushing the sand off her knees, "do you mind watching the boys for a few minutes? I've been dying to pee but I can't leave them here alone."

"I told you to go in the water. That's what we do," says Reese.

Melody shakes her head. "Only little kids can do that. Once you hit a certain age, you can get arrested."

"Really?" asks Ryan, eyes wide and finger in his nose.

"Go ahead," I tell Melody. "I'll stay here with your brothers."

"Thanks."

"Anytime," I say. And the funny thing is, I actually mean it.

MELODY

The Boy on the Beach

Confession: I don't actually need to pee. What I need is five minutes to myself. Ryan and Reese are awesome, yes. But they are exhausting. It's funny how I used to envy Katie. How even just a week ago I loved every minute of inhabiting her body. I got so lonely at my real house, but now I've come to discover that there's such a thing as too much company. It's chaos at the Miller house practically 24-7.

Reese and Ryan wake me up early every morning and they won't leave me alone until they're asleep, which seems to be happening way too late considering they're only four. I tried to talk to Katie's mom about it last night, but she immediately thought I was criticizing her. She's never around anyway. I know I made the deal, trading piano practice for babysitting, but it seems as if I'm on twin-duty nonstop, which doesn't seem exactly fair. Piano only took twenty minutes a night. I'm with Reese and Ryan for ten hours every day. Plus, Anya acts like she's doing me a favor and keeps threatening that I'm going to have to go back to the piano before the summer is over.

But I don't want to think about that right now. I am free. And I'm at the beach. It's a gorgeous day. White fluffy clouds drift lazily across the blue, blue sky. The sun shines down on my shoulders and it feels like a hug. I breathe in the sweet, salty air and step in time to the crashing of the waves.

Even though the twins are getting on my nerves, I still feel good in Katie's body. I can be myself, which is weird, since I'm not me. What I mean is that I can act like I used to, relaxed and free. Like when we were little, and I didn't have to worry about random dudes staring at me, sometimes saying creepy things, sometimes just giving creepy looks, which was often worse. Now I can let my guard down, go for a walk without worrying, and that is what I do.

That's when I see this guy walking toward me. The cool thing is, I notice him before he notices me. That never happens! Also, he's cute in a scruffy beach-rat kind of way. His dark hair is long and shaggy, clothes rumpled in that I-just-rolled-out-of-bed-and-threw-on-the-first-clean-T-shirt-I-saw way. Or maybe it's not even clean. He looks like the type of guy who wouldn't care, one way or another. He's wearing dark sunglasses, so I can't tell if he's noticing me, but I'm hoping he is.

He's getting closer and I smile at him.

He grins back and I think, *Okay, something is going to happen.* What, I don't exactly know, but for once, I actually want to be noticed—at least by this guy. And he did notice me. So whatever happens next is going to be good. I can feel it.

We're getting closer, almost close enough to talk. I'm about to say hello, but stop myself because what about Kevin?

I feel bad because, technically, I have a sweet and devoted boyfriend. What kind of girlfriend am I, being attracted to other guys?

Of course, Kevin isn't my boyfriend anymore. He's Katie's. So here I am, not tied up in any way. And this guy is standing right in front of me, smiling like he's got some big juicy secret. A secret I want him to share with me.

"Hey," I say, quickly, acting cool like I don't really care. I go to run my fingers through my curls but instead I've got Katie's straight brown hair to contend with. My fingers don't get caught and they run through too quickly.

I laugh and he does, too.

"Hi," he says back.

I've only just laid eyes on this guy—have only seen him for a total of about forty-five seconds—but I can tell I like him. In fact, I'm imagining strolling on the beach with him, hand in hand. I'll bet his hands are soft and warm and not sweaty. He won't grip me too tightly, like he'll fall off a cliff if he lets go. No, he'll be perfect at holding hands.

I wonder if he likes to text flirty messages. I'll bet he doesn't use too many emoticons while texting. I wonder what it's like to kiss him. I'll bet he doesn't apply cherry-flavored ChapStick every five seconds.

This guy doesn't smell anything like ChapStick.

"Nice day, huh?" I ask.

"The best. I love summer," he says.

"Me, too," I say. "I wish it were summer all the time. And I mean that in the strictly 'summer is fun' kind of way as opposed to 'we're all going to burn up because of global warning.'"

The guy laughs and says, "You're funny."

"Thanks," I reply. "Except I'm not funny. I'm Katie."

"You can be funny and Katie," he says. "I'm Nico."

When we shake hands I discover I was right—his skin is soft and his grip, perfect. I hold on for a few seconds too long and he seems confused as he pulls his hand away.

I giggle. "Sorry about that. Um, are you from around here?"

"Kind of. I live in West Ranch," Nico says.

"Oh, I live in Braymar. That's, like, superclose to West Ranch."

"Yeah," Nico says. "Do you go to Braymar?"

"Not yet, but soon. I'm starting seventh grade at Braymar in the fall."

"I'm going into middle school, too."

I really wish Katie could see me talking to this cute guy. She's always so hard on herself, saying that no guy would like her. Yet here I am in her body, attracting a supercute boy. It's all in her attitude, I think. Katie is a major stress-case and she's always looking down, plotting and scheming, trying to figure out what comes next. She needs to relax and live in the moment, especially in the summertime and especially at the beach. That's what I'm going to tell her as soon as I get back to our spot.

"Hey, you know that girl you were just hanging out with?" Nico asks me.

"Huh?" I ask.

"The one with the curly blond hair and that blue bikini?"

"You mean Melody?" I ask, confused.

"Yeah, Melody. You guys were talking five minutes ago, right? You left her with those two little boys."

"Yup," I say, looking over my shoulder. I can just see the three of them playing in the waves. "That's Melody and the boys are my brothers."

"Cool. Think I could get her number?" Nico asks.

Wait a minute. Why is Nico asking about my best friend when he stopped to talk to me? It doesn't make any sense. I'm all mixed up. He thinks I'm pretty. This should be a good thing. But wait—he doesn't think I'm pretty, he thinks Melody is pretty. But she didn't do anything. She's not the one who made eye contact with him. She's not the one who flirted. I am. How superficial. How great for Melody. For me. If only I were in my own body. But wait, does that make me shallow? This is so confusing.

"So can I?" he asks.

"Hey, do you actually know Melody?" I ask.

"I've seen her around," Nico says. "I mean, we've never actually spoken but I'm sure we'd get along. So what do you think?"

I put my hands on my hips. "So you're using me to get to her?" I ask in a huff.

"Well, I wouldn't put it that harshly," says Nico. "I thought you could help."

"For your information, she has a great boyfriend named Kevin. And she is very devoted to him."

Before Nico can respond, I take off and duck into the

bathroom. I know he can't follow me there and I'm too annoyed to face him.

Katie is my best friend and I miss her. And now I kind of get her. It's no fun being the sidekick to your pretty best friend.

KATIE

The Fourth

The bus to Crescent Moon Bay doesn't run on major holidays and today is the Fourth of July. Before Melody and
I switched bodies, in our first summer of being twelve,
we met Kevin in the park. At least, that's what I thought
at the time. Now I know better.

Kevin and I are already together, obviously, and it's
four o'clock and he's texting me.

'Sup? he asks. ☺ ☺ ☺ ☺ ☺ ☺

Nadda, I reply.

Want to hang? he asks. 🤙 🤙 🤙 🤙 🤙 🤙 🤙
🤙 🤙 🤙

Sure. Be right there, I text back.

I'm feeling better now that I actually have plans. We
can't get to the beach on our own without a ride, but I'm

thinking we can bike over to the park and watch the fireworks.

I wander into my gigantic walk-in closet and search for the perfect outfit. This is a challenge because I just got four new pairs of shorts. My favorite ones are dark blue with red stripes running down each side. I can't decide if they go with my new green-and-orange-polka-dot T-shirt, so I try it on. The shirt is so cute and I love the V-neck and the way it hugs Melody's body. Of course, I haven't yet worn the brown strappy sandals. I try them on, too, and look at myself in the mirror. The outfit is daring and bold. Maybe not everything goes together, but on the other hand, it's all from the same little boutique, so it must match. Right? I decide to go for it.

Puckering my lips, I apply some red lipstick and drop the tube in my new purse. It's got an American flag on it with shiny rhinestones where the stars should be— totally perfect for the holiday! Once I find my American flag dangle-y earrings I walk over to Kevin's house.

He looks at me funny when he answers the door.

"Hi, Kev," I say. I give him a quick kiss on the cheek and blush. It still feels weird, having a boyfriend. Kissing a boy. I wonder if I'll ever get used to it.

I am used to the cherry-flavored ChapStick, though. Not only used to it, I'm thoroughly tired of it. Luckily, I've learned to stand back a few feet and then I don't even smell the cherry-ness. Much.

Instead of saying hello he goes, "What are you wearing?"

"You like?" I ask, spinning around. "It's all new. Happy Fourth of July!"

"You, too," he says.

"That's all you have to say?" I ask.

And then there's this huge awkward pause.

"Tell me I look awesome," I say.

"You look awesome," Kevin repeats, his voice semi-robotic, but I can tell he doesn't mean it. Oh well. At least he said it.

And who is he to judge? Kevin is in the same shorts he's been wearing all week, plus a T-shirt advertising some soap company. No shoes. Would've been nice for him to get dressed up for me, but I don't say so. Not directly.

"Am I here too early?" I ask.

"Huh?" asks Kevin.

"I feel like I showed up before you got a chance to get dressed."

Kevin looks down at himself, confused. "Um, I am dressed, Melo. This is my favorite shirt."

"Oh," I say. "Right. Of course."

I follow him into the den, where the giant-screen TV is on. I'm figuring he's going to turn it off so we can talk, but instead he picks up his game console and continues to play.

I stand there, unsure what to do. Dating Kevin is not

what I thought it would be. It's not that he's a bad guy, exactly. He's simply not the amazing guy I thought he was. And he doesn't seem to be too into me, either.

"Have a seat," he says, patting the couch cushion beside him, not taking his eyes away from the TV.

I think maybe we're going to play together, so I sit down next to him, except he seems to be involved in a game already.

"Um, where are my controls?" I ask.

"What do you mean?" he says.

"Don't I get to play, too?"

He laughs. "Do you even know what this game is?"

It's a valid question and I answer honestly. "I don't, but I'm a fast learner."

"Sorry. I'm in the middle of playing with Buddy," he says.

Buddy is Kevin's best bud from North Carolina. He's talked about him before. And I'm all for keeping in contact with friends from home, but come on. I'm here and I'm looking fabulous in my brand-new outfit. Plus, Kevin is the one who invited me over. He can't just ignore me on a major American holiday. I cross my arms over my chest and huff.

His eyes get squinty for a moment, like he's registered my unhappiness, but he's too focused on his game to do anything about it.

I decide to huff again because maybe I wasn't loud enough the first time.

Again, he has the same nonreaction.

Maybe I need to be more direct. "Want to go to the park to see the fireworks? If we leave now I'll bet we can get a great spot. It's not about being near the front, actually. We should sit in the center and then we simply lie back and look up and we'll see everything explode above us."

Kevin doesn't reply. He's too busy pressing buttons with his fingers and moving around, flying some purple iridescent jet online, but acting like it's a real life-or-death situation.

"Do you think they'll play Katy Perry's 'Firework,' or is that too obvious?"

Kevin doesn't laugh at my excellent joke and this is too much. I stand up and turn off the TV.

He jumps up and yelps like a puppy in pain. "What are you doing? I was winning!"

"I'm not going to sit here and watch you play video games all night!" I protest.

"Who said anything about all night? I just needed to finish the game."

"Oh." That's different and now I feel bad, but this isn't my fault. "Why didn't you say so?" I ask.

"I don't know. I thought you knew," Kevin says. He takes off his hat for a moment to run one hand through his hair. "Look, I'm sorry. I'm done. What do you want to do?"

"Let's go out to dinner," I say. "We can walk to Mario's. I hear their ravioli is amazing."

"I can't go out to eat because I can't find my shoes," says Kevin.

"Are you kidding?" I ask.

"Let's order a pizza," he says.

"Okay," I say. "I love pizza."

"Me, too. Except I don't have any money on me."

I have my credit card, but Melody's mom always studies the statement and if she finds out I ate pizza again she's going to freak. I just got another lecture on healthy eating this morning because she found an empty bag of potato chips in my beach bag. We are out of luck. "I don't have any cash, either," I tell him.

"That's okay. Let's raid the fridge," says Kevin, standing up and leading me to the kitchen. He finds tortilla chips, salsa, guacamole, and a package of hot dogs.

"Yuck!" I say.

"Hot dogs are delicious," he says, grabbing one out of the package and taking a gigantic bite.

"Did you just eat that raw?" I ask.

He nods and shoves the rest of it into his mouth.

I've been a vegetarian since I was nine, and I know that's my choice and I try to respect other people's decisions, but thinking about meat grosses me out. And seeing Kevin eat a raw hot dog? "That's disgusting," I can't help but say, crinkling my nose.

"You're crazy, Melody!" He talks with his mouth full, so I smell half raw hot dog and half cherry-flavored Chap-Stick, which equals one hundred percent disgusting.

"I've gotta go," I say.

"Wait, are you mad?" he asks. "Don't be mad, Melo."

"I'm not mad," I say, backing away. "I'm just, um, I've gotta go."

"Can we do something on Sunday? It's supposed to be an awesome day for waves."

"I don't want to go to the beach and sit on the sand for six hours and watch you surf," I say.

"Oh," says Kevin. "Okay, that's cool. We can do something else. How about we go to the mall?"

"Okay," I agree, even though I just went to the mall yesterday. Melody's mom and I bought everything worth buying at the mall.

But hanging out there with Kevin is a whole different thing. It's got to be, because Kevin is the guy of my dreams . . . right?

MELODY

Spaghetti Mess

Fourth of July was amazing! Anya, Jeff, Reese, and Ryan and I played Wiffle ball at McClaren Park and then had a picnic while the sun set. Once it was dark we marveled as the fireworks lit up the night sky. I'm just sorry Katie missed it. I would've invited her but we haven't spoken since we ran into each other at the beach. It's weird. Anyway, I'm sure she and Kevin had better plans.

Now it's Saturday night and Katie's parents have a date night. That means Katie is stuck home babysitting. Stuck home is what she always said about it, except as usual, she was being way negative. Not everyone needs to go out every night of her life. There are plenty of things to do at home. Especially when you live in a cozy home with two cute stepbrothers. We can bake cookies. We can tie-dye T-shirts. We can make play dough because I downloaded a cool recipe on Katie's laptop. Or we can do it all. We've got tons of time and I'm excited.

Katie's mom and Jeff are going to take a cooking class: vegetarian Indian food. It sounds fun. I love Indian food and I'm a vegetarian now, so what could be better?

Katie's mom lets me help her pick out her outfit and jewelry, which is totally fun. My mom never lets me help her with stuff like that. She emerges from her room perfectly coiffed every single night, as if she has invisible elf stylists hidden in a secret compartment in her jewelry box.

Who knows? Maybe she does. It's not my problem tonight.

I'm sitting on the edge of Anya's bed as she pulls clothes out of her closet.

"Does this shirt make me look like I'm old but trying to look young?" she asks me, holding up a silky blue tank.

"No, and that top is so cute," I tell her. "Can I borrow it sometime?"

She hands it to me. "Take it. It's yours now because I think I made my point!"

Three outfit changes later she settles on a red, yellow, and blue caftan with white capri pants and cute high-heel sandals, light brown like a worn-in saddle on a horse. She also puts on the new charm necklace Jeff bought her.

There are three charms on it: one for Katie, one for Reese, and one for Ryan. I love how she wears her whole family around her neck—like she's always thinking about us, which she so totally is.

When Anya is ready she spins around and asks me what I think.

"You look amazing," I tell her, and I'm being honest. Anya looks supercute and vibrant. She's not obsessed with being rail thin and hard bodied like my mom. She's a little chubby and she lets herself eat cake. She doesn't always wear makeup and when she does, it's only lipstick. Even tonight on date night. She's worried about being old but she looks adorable. I can totally see Anya and Jeff together in middle school. They are goofy and in love. It's no wonder Katie feels so much pressure to meet a boy. If my parents were this happy, I'd want to meet a boy, too. And honestly, I kind of do want to meet a boy. A boy other than my boyfriend . . .

As soon as we head downstairs Reese and Ryan run up to me. "What are we going to do?" Reese asks.

"Well, that depends," I say, explaining about the play-dough recipe and the tie-dye.

Ryan looks at Reese and makes a face.

"Or we can start a new book. Have you guys ever read *Matilda*?"

"We've seen the movie," Reese says with a yawn.

I look to Anya, hoping she'll help me, but she's applying lipstick in the front hall mirror, pretending like she doesn't hear.

"Can't we watch a movie?" Ryan asks.

"Please, please, please," says Reese.

There's no reason Anya should say no, as far as I'm concerned. It's summertime. The kids and I played outside all day and I'm tired. Last night we had an awesome picnic at the beach. We hike every Saturday and have been running around nonstop. What's wrong with vegging in front of the TV every once in a while?

Except as I'm pleading my case, Jeff comes into the room and interrupts, saying, "No TV. Make sure you give the boys a bath. And please wash their hair tonight. There's plenty of food in the fridge for dinner. They can have pasta or hot dogs or both, but don't forget about the vegetables. There's cut-up cucumbers and carrots on the top shelf. Bedtime is at seven thirty sharp."

"I only like carrots, not cucumbers," says Reese.

"And seven thirty is way too early!" Ryan yells.

"That's perfectly acceptable," says Jeff. "Right, Katie?"

"Listen to your sister, boys," Anya says. "She's in charge."

And then they are gone.

The three of us watch them walk to the curb and get into Jeff's old Subaru. Then as soon as they pull away the boys hoot with delight and start tearing apart the living room couch. It's instant chaos.

"What are you guys doing?" I ask.

"Making a fort!" Reese says, like it's obvious. Every couch cushion is now on the floor. Ryan is pushing the coffee table out of the way.

"Is this allowed?" I ask.

"Duh. Of course it is," says Reese.

"Then why did you only start building the fort after your parents walked out the door?" I ask.

The boys look at me guiltily.

I answer my own question. "Because you aren't allowed."

"It's fine as long as you clean it up when we go to bed, because last time we got in trouble," Ryan tells me.

"Wait, it's not my job to clean this up," I say.

The boys giggle mischievously as they bean each other with pillows.

"This isn't fort building. This is fighting, which is definitely not allowed," I say.

The boys ignore me and I give up. I'm tired from this morning's hike. Plus, Ryan and Reese woke me up at five thirty yesterday because they wanted help building a garage for their Matchbox cars. The morning before that, they wanted to play superheroes at six.

I head into the den. The piano looms large in the

corner like a threat. Anya said my weeks of trading piano practice for babysitting were over. I told Anya the piano is way out of tune and playing it in this condition would be bad for me. She actually bought the excuse, and now I don't have to practice until they get it fixed, but the repair guy is coming next week. I don't know what I'm going to do after that.

Suddenly I hear a crash and a yell. I run into the living room to find Ryan in tears. Worse—both boys are hitting each other but not with pillows. They are using their fists.

"Break it up!" I yell, pulling them apart. "What is going on?"

Ryan says, "Reese pushed me into a wall."

"It was an accident," says Reese. "He hit me for no reason."

"Cut it out," I yell. "And be more careful."

They pull away from me and continue with the pillow fight.

I wonder how much Katie gets paid to babysit. Since it's a weekend, and not an official piano-practice trade, I assume I'll make some cash. I just hope it's enough for a new bathing suit. I'm not crazy about any of Katie's. They are all superskimpy bikinis, and whenever I swim in a bikini, my stomach gets cold and I stress about a giant wave crashing down and washing away my suit. Simple tanks make so much more sense.

I wander back upstairs to my room and try to read. I went to the library and got some new books yesterday. But it's way too loud. I can't focus.

I wonder how long an Indian cooking class lasts. Jeff and Anya have to drive there, which is twenty minutes, minimum. And the class has to last for at least an hour—maybe two. After they cook they get to eat what they've made, which means another forty-five minutes, maybe? I'm sure they'll be home to relieve me at any moment. I glance at my clock. It reads 6:05.

That means Anya and Jeff have only been gone for ten minutes.

"Hey, what's for dinner?" Reese asks, coming into my room without knocking.

"Great question," I say. I head downstairs to the kitchen and check the fridge. I see the carrots and cucumbers Jeff mentioned and also the macaroni and cheese and hot dogs. Yum. Hot dogs. They look delicious, so now I have this moral dilemma. Katie is a vegetarian and I am occupying Katie's body. Does that mean I have to be a vegetarian, too? Is it disrespectful to eat a hot dog? Or can I do whatever I want now that I'm her?

She's probably hanging out with my boyfriend at the moment, for instance. They may have even kissed. And I don't mind. I am happy to have time off from Kevin. I should probably break up with him, but we are not broken up yet. So is my boyfriend cheating on me with my best friend? Or is my best friend simply being faithful to our switch? Can both things be true?

And back to the original, most pressing question, can I eat the hot dog?

My stomach is growling, which means my body is telling me to eat it. The real Katie will never know. It's totally okay.

I take a small bite.

"What are you doing?" asks Ryan.

"Nothing!" I say, hiding the rest of the hot dog behind my back. "Nothing at all."

"You ate a hot dog," says Ryan.

"It's a veggie dog," I lie. "And I only took a bite."

Ryan looks at me funny. He's on to me—I can tell. "It's a regular hot dog and you're not Katie," he says.

I giggle out of nervousness. "Why do you keep saying that, little dude?" I ask, ruffling his hair.

"*You* don't call me little dude," he says. "Melody does."

This is true. I can't believe how perceptive he is. Or maybe I can. Kids are geniuses. It's only when they grow up that their senses get dulled. Like the adults in the world, they start caring about things that don't matter. Then things they used to know they suddenly don't anymore. The doubt creeps in.

"You're not Katie and Melody is not Melody. Everything is mixed up!" he says.

I am amazed and scared.

"Look, squirt," I say, in my best imitation of Katie. "Leave me alone, okay? I've got better things to do than argue with you about stuff that doesn't make any sense."

Ryan frowns at me like he's seeing through me, and then Reese bursts into the room. "I'm starving!" he groans. "You're supposed to be making us dinner."

"Okay, but you need to chill out," I reply. And I'm not even channeling Katie anymore. I'm genuinely annoyed. "What do you guys want?"

"Spaghetti!" Ryan yells.

"Why not mac and cheese?" I ask, showing them the glass container. "It's already made, so I'll heat it up."

"No, we had that last night," says Reese. "I want spaghetti, too."

"Okay, if you guys insist," I say. Spaghetti sounds easy, which puts me in a better mood. I don't really cook, but I'm sure I can handle this. I find the package in the cupboard and some sauce in the fridge. Perfect.

I read the instructions on the pasta. Apparently I must *bring water to a rolling boil*. But what does that even mean?

The boys are staring at me, which is adding pressure. It makes me feel like I'm gonna mess something up.

"Guys, go play, okay? I'll let you know when everything is ready."

They take off.

I gulp and open five cabinets before I find the right pot. I fill it with water and put it on the stove. Then I turn it on. The flame jumps up from the burner like magic. Lovely.

I turn it to high because I can't let the twins starve on my watch.

Except when I stare at the water, nothing seems to be happening. I find the lid and put it on. This should make it heat up faster, right? Yes. That makes total sense. This cooking-dinner thing is a snap. I should do it more often.

It sounds as if the boys have resumed their fort building/pillow fighting and they're having so much fun I decide to join them. I grab a throw pillow and knock Ryan down and he falls into Reese and the boys topple like silly, giggly dominoes.

Then Reese gets up and knocks me in the head, but it doesn't hurt. We are all smiles. I love these boys. We are having a blast. Babysitting is fun!

A few minutes later, I hear something strange and it seems to be coming from the kitchen—a weird sizzling type of noise.

Uh-oh.

I run back to find the water has boiled over onto the stove and the flames are shooting up high. I grab the pot and yell, "*YEEEOUCH!!!!*" I let go and shake out my throbbing hand. I've burned myself. And the water is still bubbling over.

I turn off the flame with my good hand. Meanwhile, my burned fingers are red and swollen. They hurt so, so much that tears spring to my eyes.

"Where's dinner?" asks Reese.

"We're starving!" yells Ryan.

I take a deep, shaky breath. "Hold on guys," I manage to gasp. "I need a minute."

Okay, I tell myself. Don't cry in front of the boys. Don't cry in front of the boys. If they see you cry, they'll get scared and that's not good for anyone. I sniff and take another breath and run my throbbing red fingers under cold water. It helps a little.

After that I turn the stove back on, add the spaghetti to the pot, and set the table.

Eight minutes later the pasta looks done. I drain it, careful to use the oven mitts this time, and put it back in the pot and pour the sauce on top, stirring. I'm so proud. While only incurring a minor injury, I have made spaghetti and it looks delicious.

When I go to get the boys, the living room is a feathery mess. "It looks like a chicken exploded in here!" I scream.

The boys collapse into fits of giggles.

"You're so funny now, Katie," Ryan says.

Normally their laughs are infectious. Now I am annoyed, though. What will Jeff and Anya say? Will they blame the exploded pillow on me? Probably.

"Dinner is ready," I say. "Come on."

The boys run into the kitchen and I'm proud of what I've done. Spaghetti and red sauce, and I even set the table with a fancy, red-checked tablecloth and matching napkins. Their sippy cups are filled with apple juice and everything looks lovely.

Reese sits down and starts to eat but Ryan is standing over his chair, about to cry.

"What's wrong?" I ask.

"I hate red sauce," he tells me. "I wanted butter and cheese!"

"Why didn't you say so?" I ask.

"Because I usually don't have to. If you were really Katie, you'd know."

He's sobbing and I'm not sure what to say. This is so superstressful.

"I am really Katie. Never mind, Ryan. Of course I'll make you new spaghetti. I just forgot. It's been kind of a crazy day."

"Can I have orange juice instead of apple?" asks Reese.

"Apple juice is yuck. I want chocolate milk," says Ryan.

"Oh, me, too," Reese says as soon as I finish pouring his juice.

This is impossible!

Two hours later, the boys are bathed and in pajamas and sleeping upstairs. I'm collapsed in Katie's bed, staring at the ceiling. I'm too tired to read, too tired to sleep, too tired to move.

At 10:15 I hear the door open up. Jeff and Anya walk in, giggling.

Then a few moments later Anya calls, "Are you still awake, Katie?"

I drag myself out of bed and head to the top of the steps. "Hi, did you guys have fun?" I ask, peering down.

Anya is looking at the mess, not happy. "What happened to the living room?" she asks.

"The boys made a fort," I say. "They didn't get a chance to clean it up before bedtime but they promised they would in the morning."

"Katie, we talked about this," says Anya.

"We did?" I ask, because this is news to me.

Anya sighs. "You know the kids aren't allowed to build forts on weekends."

"Oh, right, but I don't get why. If they can build forts sometimes, then why not whenever they want to? It doesn't make any sense."

"It makes sense because it's a rule that Jeff and I came up with. You can't change the rules around here. That's not your job."

"Okay," I say, wondering why I'm getting a lecture. I sacrificed my whole night, took care of the boys, and did an awesome job of it, if I do say so myself. Meanwhile, Jeff and Anya haven't even thanked me. But that's okay. "I'll definitely remember that the next time I babysit," I tell them, checking my watch. "You guys have been gone for over four hours, wow! That's a long time. Um, I can't remember—what's my usual rate?"

Jeff squints up at me, confused. "You don't get paid to take care of your brothers," he says.

"Wait. You're kidding, right?" I ask. "This wasn't a piano-practice trade. We already finished with that. And it's a Saturday night. I just figured—"

"Oh, Katie. We've been over this so many times," says Anya, sounding tired.

I am shocked. "Are you telling me that Katie babysits for free?"

"It's not babysitting, Katie," says Jeff. "And why are you talking about yourself in the third person?"

"I'm not." I cough. "I mean, I babysit for free. All the time. So, um, can we go over this again? Why do I always have to babysit for free?"

"We're a family," says Anya. "You don't get paid for spending time with your family."

KATIE

Hanging at the Mall

As soon as I wake up on Sunday I choose another spectacular outfit: a leopard-print tank top with zebra-striped capris because of course all animal prints go together. Since the mall is overly air-conditioned I also snag Debbie's faux-fur vest. At least I hope it's faux . . .

Kevin and I are meeting at the mall because he's got to have brunch with his dad and some of their cousins. I take Melody's fancy ten-speed and get there with barely enough time to get to our meeting spot at the Gap.

As I stand there I realize that Kevin never specified whether he meant GapKids or GapBody or plain old Gap for grown-ups and teenagers. It would make sense, if you owned the Gap, to put all of your Gaps in one place at the mall, but for some reason that's not what they did.

GapKids is downstairs and it's attached to babyGap. Gap-Body is on level three, next to Victoria's Secret. And plain old regular Gap is tucked into the corner next to a giant department store on the second floor. That's where I'm waiting. And I keep checking Melody's phone but Kevin hasn't responded to any of my texts. He's fifteen minutes late.

Maybe I'll write a letter to the head of the Gap. Except that's something I'd do as Katie, not as Melody. Melody would simply shrug her shoulders and say, "Oh well. That's just how it is."

She doesn't like to criticize. I never understood why. It's not like Melody has nothing to say. She's got lots to say. She simply doesn't bother to actually say things out loud, usually. Even things that are important to her.

She used to take this painting class a few years ago and she really loved it but it was all the way on the other side of town and it got in the way of her mom's favorite spin class. Debbie talked Melody into quitting. "It's not like you're going to be an artist anyway," she said. And Melody went along with it. She never complained out loud, but I know it bothered her. Because guess what? Melody loves art and she's supertalented, too. Like she might grow up to be an artist if she wants to be.

She used to constantly sketch stuff when we were

younger and then she stopped, I thought for good. But I think she's actually been drawing in secret now.

I was going through her drawer last night and found an entire notebook filled with her drawings and most of them are really good. I don't know why she never showed them to me.

Glancing at my watch, I can now see that Kevin is twenty minutes late. This is unacceptable.

I look around and notice I'm standing two doors down from Color Me Lovely. Melody and I only went once. It must've been four or five years ago, I can't remember exactly. What I do remember is that we made platters. Melody insisted and I don't know why. Mine was kind of boring. The problem is that I can't draw, so I made it blue. And my mom and Jeff actually use it, which is kind of embarrassing. I mean, it's a dumb blue platter I made, and it even has a chip in it, but they don't care. They act like it's so great but I secretly think the issue is that we can't afford to get a new, nonchipped platter.

Melody's platter was amazing. If I were her mom I'd use it every day. Except I've been living in her house for weeks and I haven't seen it anywhere.

Anyway, I'm standing here in front of regular old Gap, still waiting for Kevin, checking my phone for an apology text that hasn't yet come. And this guy comes over to me and asks, "Need some help?"

I look up. He's tall and his shoulders are wide. He's wearing a red baseball cap and a red T-shirt with jeans. He's cute but way too old to be paying any attention to me. I bet he's in high school. He may even be a senior in high school. He definitely looks old enough to drive. And in fact, he's got car keys hanging out of his jeans pocket.

I don't know why he's asking if I need help. I'm standing here minding my own business. "No. I'm fine." I smile to be polite but he takes that as an invitation to stick around when all I want is for him to leave me alone.

"Doing some shopping today?" he asks.

"I'm waiting for my boyfriend, actually," I say.

The dude grins. "If you were my girlfriend, no way would I make you wait."

I look around, even more annoyed, wishing Kevin would get here already.

"I'm JJ," the dude tells me, holding out his hand.

"Melody," I say. I don't shake his hand. I don't want to be rude but I don't want to be too nice, either.

I don't love the attention. I don't even *like* it because it makes me so uncomfortable. Next time I check my phone it falls out of my hand and I bend down to pick it up. JJ does, too, and we bump foreheads and then I shout, "Ouch!" And I'm loud about it. Not simply because it hurts, although it does, but also because I'm furious with my boyfriend for not being here, for leaving me alone to deal with this annoying guy.

"Oh no. You okay? I'm so sorry," JJ says. He's holding on to my arms and I don't want him to, so I shake him off, and now here comes Kevin. Finally! When it's too late.

"Hey, what's up?" Kevin asks me, looking from me to the guy and then back to me, again, confused. I get it. If I walked up to Kevin and found some random girl half hugging him I'd be weirded out, too. But I am too angry to say anything.

"She's with you?" JJ asks Kevin, like I'm a trombone or a bicycle or a puppy dog.

Kevin stands up straighter and puts his arm around me, pulling me closer. "Yup."

He kisses me on the cheek.

JJ waves and walks away.

I wipe off the waxy residue but my cheek stays sticky and smelly.

"What's wrong?" he asks me.

I guess it's obvious I'm supercranky.

"Nothing," I tell him. But what I actually mean is, *everything*.

I thought dating Kevin would be different. I thought we'd be elevated to a whole new social stratosphere. I thought we'd go to movies, take romantic walks on the beach, and have candlelit dinners at fancy restaurants. But instead here we are at the mall. And I'm kind of bored.

Crazy thing is, I actually miss my real family, and the constant hiking followed by breakfast at Jinkey's. I'm missing the smell of blueberry jam and the stickiness of the twins. I'm even missing being smushed between their car seats and having them wake me up crazy early to look at their Lego creations or to help them blow their noses or whatever.

Kevin says, "You're acting weird, Melo."

"Sorry," I say. "It's been a weird day."

"I'm not talking about today. I mean in general. You've been weird for weeks."

I don't know how to respond, because he's right but I can't say why. We walk in silence for a while. I try to enjoy the moment, try to remind myself that I am hanging out at the mall with my gorgeous boyfriend, with my perfect body and perfect life. I have everything I've ever wanted, yet somehow it doesn't feel like I thought it would.

Soon we run into a few of Kevin's surfer buddies: Sanjay, Han, and Avi. Kevin gives them high fives. He's always high-fiving everyone.

"What are you dudes up to?" he asks.

"We're about to see the new Vin Diesel movie," says Avi.

"Oh, killer," says Kevin. He looks at me with his eye-brows raised, like asking permission to go.

"We saw it last week," I remind him. But why do I even need to? He knows this. The entire movie was one two-hour chase scene with tons of explosions and noise. He thought it was the best thing he'd ever seen. I could barely keep my eyes open. Afterward we went out for ice cream and I tried to figure out why he thought the movie was so awesome, but all he could say was, "It just was." And I kept pressing him because I really wanted to understand, but he finally got annoyed and said, "Don't think about it so much, Melody."

And that was that.

"Want to go again?" he asks me now. "Maybe you'll like it better the second time?"

"Are you seriously asking me to sit through that garbage again?" I huff, crankier than ever.

His friends hold up their hands and laugh, saying, "Whoa, Melo. Not so mellow today."

It's true. I'm not so mellow. I don't want to be Melo Melody anymore. Melo Melody doesn't get what she wants and she gets walked all over.

"Guess the old lady says no," Kevin says.

After his friends move on, Kevin tries to grab my hand but I don't let him.

"What was that?" I ask.

"Huh?" Kevin says.

"Did you really call me your old lady?"

"Oh, I was only joking around with my bros."

"They are not your bros. They're guys you surf with."

"Yeah, but we're tight," says Kevin.

"Know what? Why don't you go to the movie with them if you guys are so tight? I'll hang out here on my own."

Obviously I don't mean this. I expect Kevin to apologize and say, "No way, Melody. We had plans. I'd never ditch you to hang out with some random surfer dudes. And by the way, sorry I was late meeting you and you look awesome in that new outfit."

Except he doesn't say any of that. Instead he goes, "Okay, thanks." And he kisses me on the cheek and takes off, leaving me alone at the mall.

I am alone at the mall.

This was not supposed to happen.

I storm out the front doors, unlock my bike, and ride home. When Kevin comes by later on tonight, I'm totally going to give him a hard time.

Except Kevin doesn't come by tonight.

He doesn't show up the next night, either.

And actually, he doesn't even contact me for three days after that. And when he does? All he does is text.

K: **U missed an awesome movie.**

I ignore him.

Melo?

You there?

Hello?

He sends me some emoticons with smiley faces and hearts and a hand delivering flowers. Real flowers would be cool. I've never gotten any from a boy before, except for my father and he doesn't count, obviously. But emoticon flowers? That takes zero effort! I am not impressed.

I am so over this. I turn off my phone. Debbie is out again, so I head to the kitchen in search of a snack. The only thing vaguely appealing is kale chips. They are green and kind of furry, too. Still, desperate times call for desperate measures. I take a bite. I make a face. They are not delicious. Still, they are my only option. And if I close my eyes and crunch they at least sound a little bit like potato chips. I finish the whole bag.

Later that night there's a knock on my door.

It's Kevin.

"What do you want?" I ask.

"I wanted to make sure you're okay. I haven't heard from you in a while."

"I can't believe you ditched me at the mall," I say.

"Ditched you? I invited you to come with me."

"And I didn't want to go!"

"Right, and I did," says Kevin with a shrug. "So it's a win-win."

"It's not a win-win. We had plans. We were supposed to hang out."

"Well, we can hang out now." Kevin smiles and tries to high-five me but I ignore his outstretched hand.

"No, thanks," I say. "I'm kind of tired."

"I'm going surfing tomorrow," he says. "Want to watch?"

I don't, actually. I want Kevin to be different. I want him to be the guy I thought he was before I knew him. But it's not like I can ask for that.

Rocket Ship Dogs

I don't know why, but I wake up a few days later thinking about Color Me Lovely again. Not the store, exactly, though. I'm thinking about my platter.

You can't take stuff home from Color Me Lovely right after you paint it. Everything has to be glazed and fired so it'll last forever. And that can take days or sometimes even a week. Katie and I didn't get to pick up our platters until the following Saturday.

I remember the moment when I saw my finished work, how my chest swelled with pride.

Katie's mom had driven us to the mall that day and I could see she was impressed with my work. "This is extraordinary," she said. "You are really talented, Melody."

"Check out mine," Katie said, muscling her way in

front of me and thrusting her plain blue platter into her mother's hands.

"Well, that's lovely, too," said Anya. "It's a nice classic color. We can use this."

Anya winked at me like we shared a secret. And we did. Maybe it seems mean and competitive, I don't know. But I was so used to Katie being better at everything—school, piano, and life in general. She always got what she wanted, was never afraid to stand up for herself. It meant a lot to me to know that my platter was better. That Anya thought I was talented.

That night I took the platter home and presented it to my parents at dinner. Back then we used to have family dinners on occassion.

Both of them *ooh*ed and *aah*ed over the platter, like it was the most amazing thing I'd ever made. And it was.

"This is incredible," my mom said. "Lovely. I'm so proud of you, Melody."

"Maybe you have a future as an artist," said my dad.

Kyle laughed and said, "She probably used stencils to make those things. They're too perfect."

"I did not use stencils," I said, annoyed even though a small part of me gloated over the fact that he assumed I needed extra help to make the images look so good.

"Whatever," Kyle mumbled, scowling as usual.

My mom said, "Well, either way, it's lovely, Melo. Your

color choices are beautiful. You have an amazing eye. Maybe we should redo the den in this palette."

"I didn't use stencils," I repeated, except no one was listening anymore.

My parents were back to talking about the kitchen remodel and where we'd go for Christmas—Hawaii again or Jackson Hole for some skiing?

Someone put the platter in the back of a cabinet and I never saw it again.

I don't know why this is all coming up now. Maybe because my life is so much better now that I'm Katie. I'm the oldest and I've got two brothers, both of them sweethearts.

It's six o'clock in the morning and I can hear them playing Rocket Ship Dogs downstairs. It's a game we invented last night. The boys pretend to be dogs on rocket ships, zooming through space in search of gigantic atomic bones. It was fun the first time we played, but now, at this early hour? Not so much.

I roll over and bury my head under my pillow. I can still hear them barking, but it's a little better this way. And even though they woke me up, I'm happy to hear them playing with the dog masks I made for them last night. I love drawing dogs. I love drawing, period.

Soon my door opens a crack and Anya peeks her head in.

"Hey, Katie? Do you mind going downstairs and telling the boys to stop whatever they're doing? They're being way too loud and we had a really late night."

I sit up in my bed, stunned and speechless. I know they had a late night. I babysat for the boys. Again. For free!

And I had a late night, too. I fell asleep in front of the TV. TV I wasn't supposed to be watching, as Anya and Jeff both told me when they woke me up. But that's beside the point.

I should be allowed to watch a little television. It's summer. I've babysat for five nights in a row. And I'm tired, too. I should be allowed to sleep. Ryan and Reese are not my kids. In fact, I'm kind of a kid, too. I need my rest. But I don't say any of this. Instead, I throw back the covers and wander downstairs.

"Hey, guys?" I whisper. "Let's play a new game. It's called superquiet bunnies."

KATIE

Kyle Comes Home

It's August first and Kyle is on break from his summer classes. He's home for two whole days and I'm excited because this house is getting lonely. Especially since Kevin and I are no longer speaking. We had this whole fight last night about how he's not being the boyfriend he's supposed to be. And according to him, I've changed in a major way, too. I had to pretend to not know what he was talking about, even though of course I do.

Obviously I am no mellow Melody. But I look like her and I sound like her and I live in her house. I've been able to fool everyone else, so Kevin doesn't know what he's talking about. At least I hope he doesn't. I don't know what'll happen if anyone finds out about my switch with Melody. Nothing good, I am sure. So it's totally for the best that Kevin and I are taking a break.

Debbie and I are speeding on the freeway, on our way to pick up Kyle at the airport. The music is blasting way too loud and we don't attempt to talk. She's in an awful mood and I'm afraid to say a word. I heard Debbie yelling on the phone this morning, fighting with Melody's dad because he's not home yet. When she hung up I asked her if everything was okay and she said, "Fine," not wanting to talk. I probably shouldn't have asked. I probably should've pretended I hadn't heard a thing.

By the time we get to the airport Kyle is curbside with his shiny silver suitcase next to him. He's wearing jeans and a shirt with a collar, tucked in. His hair is slicked back and his glasses are oversize. On some people they'd look cute and trendy, but Kyle looks like an extra in the remake of *Revenge of the Nerds*. At least he's not wearing a pocket protector. He looks younger than how I remember him and not exactly happy, maybe because we're so late.

I jump out of the car as soon as Debbie puts it into park and wrap my arms around him. "Kyle!" I yell. "Sorry to keep you waiting, bro. Great to see you."

He doesn't hug me back and seems totally freaked out. "What did you call me?" he asks.

"Bro," I reply. Then I take a few steps away because

clearly this isn't how Melody would do things. Still, I can't help but add, "I've missed you."

"Why?" he asks. "It's not like you need help with homework. It's still summer, last I checked. Unless you failed sixth grade and need to go to summer school."

I can't tell if Kyle's joking or not. If so, it's not funny. If not, it's pretty mean. Either way, I can't think of a good response.

Debbie is out of the car and opening the trunk. She must've heard what he said and I expect her to leap to my defense, but the only thing she says is, "Welcome back, Kyle." Then she leans in to give him a quick kiss on the cheek.

They are the same height and they have the same eyes, too—icy-cold blue.

Kevin hoists his suitcase into the trunk and it barely fits.

Debbie slams the trunk closed and gets back into the driver's seat, leaving me and Kyle on the curb.

I wait for Kyle to get into the backseat.

Kyle waits for me to crawl in back.

"I've just been on a plane for six hours in coach. I'm sitting in front," Kyle says. He has a point, but he doesn't have to be so rude about it.

"Why are you being so mean?" I ask.

Kyle looks at me, completely shocked. "This is how I always act," he says.

I am not sure how to reply. I knew Melody and Kyle didn't get along so well, but I never realized things were this bad.

"Can you stop fighting and get in the car?" Debbie asks. "We need to get on the freeway before rush hour."

I huff and climb into the backseat. Kyle and Melody were never superclose. Kyle is a guy who keeps to himself, doing his own mysterious genius-big-brother thing. But I can't figure out why he's so prickly. It makes no sense. Melody is his little sister and he hasn't seen her—me—in ages.

Debbie asks, "How's school?" as she pulls away from the curb.

"Fine," says Kyle. Then he turns up the radio and pulls out his phone and starts to text.

"Um, are we going out for dinner or eating at home?" I ask. I'm hoping we get to go out. There's no good food at Melody's house. At the same time, though, whenever we go out Debbie watches me like a hawk and usually criticizes my order. It's kind of a lose-lose situation.

"I'm not hungry," Debbie says. "You kids can do whatever you want."

"I have plans," says Kyle.

When we get back to the house, Kyle heads for his room and slams the door closed behind him. Debbie goes to her room and does the same. I am hungry, so I head to the kitchen and rifle through the cabinets in search of something delicious. As usual, I don't find a thing that I actually want to eat—only packages of chia seeds, quinoa, and brown rice. Luckily, though, there's a fancy-looking gift basket hidden in the back of the fridge behind the celery sticks. I pull it out and unwrap it, finding crackers and a wedge of smoked cheddar cheese. It's delicious.

Soon Debbie joins me in the kitchen. "Want one?" I ask, offering her the box of crackers.

"No, thanks," she says, sitting at the counter with a magazine. "And don't eat too many of those."

"I won't," I say with my mouth full.

Debbie rolls her eyes.

Then something crazy happens. Nick, Melody's dad, appears and kisses me on the head. "Hi, sweetie. How've you been?"

"Great," I say. And wait for another question, or something, because he hasn't been around for the entire summer. This is the first time I've seen the guy. But another question doesn't come.

He and Debbie don't even say hello. Suddenly it feels very chilly in this kitchen.

Soon Debbie stands and heads to the top of the steps and yells, "Kyle, your father's home!"

Kyle comes downstairs and he and his dad shake hands and make small talk. Now we're all in the kitchen together. Except Nick still hasn't kissed Debbie hello and she barely acknowledges his presence. She doesn't even look up from the fashion magazine she's flipping through.

"Look, Debbie. I don't think I can make it for dinner tonight, okay? I'm exhausted," Nick says.

"Kyle's got plans, anyway, but remember, he's only here for two nights," says Debbie.

"Let's try for tomorrow," Nick says as he loosens his tie. "I'll make reservations somewhere good."

"I can't tomorrow night," says Kyle.

He takes a handful of crackers and shoves them in his mouth. Then he polishes off the rest of the cheese. Debbie watches but doesn't tell him to be careful of carbs or whatever. She doesn't say a word about what he's eating and this annoys me.

Nick's smile is too stiff, too wide, like he's in pain. "How's school?"

"Good," says Kyle.

"Keeping up the grades?"

"Of course," says Kyle. He's looking at his cell phone, hardly paying attention to his dad, but no one seems to mind.

A minute later Nick gets a call, and wanders out of the room to take it.

Everyone else leaves, too.

I finish the crackers and head upstairs into Melody's

room. It's messy now, something Debbie isn't happy about. But I like it—it looks more lived in. This whole house is too perfect-looking considering how imperfect things are. Melody never said a word about what it's really like around here. Or maybe she tried to but I refused to hear it. I was so convinced she was the lucky one because she's so pretty and surrounded by so much pretty stuff. I'd no idea what her life was really like.

I gaze at myself in the full-length mirror attached to the back of the closet door. My blond curls are silky smooth and bouncy. I've got big green eyes and a curvy grown-up body. I can see how this is a problem. People only seeing what's on the outside. I've got a lot going on inside. Melody does, too. She's smart and a great artist and she's holding it together in this messed-up family. How is she always so cheerful and sweet and optimistic? I wish I could ask her.

I hear a thunderclap that shakes the whole house. Looking outside, I see lightning, then more thunder and then rain—sheets and sheets of it.

Whenever it rained when we were younger, Melody would run outside and move the snails and earthworms out of harm's way, hiding them under hedges and what-not. She was protecting them from Kyle, she said, who'd step on them simply to hear the crunch of their shells and to see the gooeyness on the bottom of his shoe. I always thought she was joking. Now I'm not so sure.

Kyle is grown up now but he still seems like the type of guy who'd step on snails for fun. I wonder why Melody didn't ever tell me how bad things were. How rude her brother is and how weird her mom is about stuff. And how her dad's just absent . . .

It's cold in this house and I'm not talking about the temperature. Tonight Melody's house is full, meaning everyone is home. Yet it's supersilent. Everyone is in separate rooms, no one talking or interacting. It's weird and I feel kind of trapped. Imprisoned in this body. I miss the smell of peanut butter and blueberry jam. I'd make myself a sandwich if I could, except there is no jam in this house. It's too high in sugar.

I'm sick of green smoothies for breakfast.

I want real food, but that's not it.

I know I used to make fun of Melody and her pretend problems, but now I see how unfair I've been. Her problems are real, and worse than that, her problems are now my problems.

As I stare out at the rain I realize I'm close to tears.

I miss the real Melody.

I miss my mom and Jeff and Reese and Ryan, too.

I miss my messy, imperfect life. And more than anything else, I want to go home.

MELODY

Back on the Bus

The twins keep begging me to bring them to the beach even though I just took them four days ago. I don't have it in me to wrangle with them again. Not today. I love the boys, but they are intense and exhausting and I need some space because they are driving me bananas. Anya and Jeff are, too. It's been fun being part of a big happy family, but the Millers are not perfect. No family is. My own included, but I still miss them.

My plan is to take the beach bus solo, get to Crescent Moon Bay, and go for a long walk. Being at the beach always makes me feel better, and summer is practically over.

When I step onto the bus I'm surprised to see someone in my regular seat. Me. I mean Katie in my body.

As soon as Katie spots me, she gives me a little smile.

"Hey. Are you waiting for Kevin?" I ask.

"No," she says, looking out the window. "I'm here on my own."

"Oh. Me, too." I'm standing over her awkwardly and I should probably move on and find a seat, but I don't want to.

"Um, want to sit down?" she asks, moving her backpack to make room.

A wave of relief rushes through me as I take the seat.

It's funny, being here next to Katie on the beach bus. It feels like the beginning of summer, I mean other than the fact that we are in each other's bodies. Everything else is the same. The bus has the same old salami-and-baked-sweat smell, and my thighs are already sticking to the seats. Last night's rain cleared away the smog, so I can see the mountains in the distance. I've missed Katie, I realize. Missed what could've been a fun adventure for us if only we'd stuck together.

As the bus pulls away from the curb I ask, "How've you been?"

I expect Katie to gloat and tell me how fabulous she is and how she's absolutely thrilled to be living my life. But she doesn't say any of that. Instead she starts to cry.

KATIE

Tears and Fears

Something about seeing Melody in my body gets me choked up inside and I can't help but be superemotional.

"What's wrong?" she asks, worried.

"Nothing," I say. I try to wipe away the tears but they keep coming and they keep coming fast. "Everything! I am so happy to see you." I give Melody a huge hug. I am shaking—I can't help myself. "Can we be friends again? I've missed you so much. I'm sorry for being bossy. I'm sorry for telling you your life is perfect. It is so not perfect."

She pulls back and stares straight at me. "What's going on?" she asks.

As the bus moves away from the curb I tell her everything—all about the workouts and the shopping, and the lousy visit with Kyle, and Kevin's cherry-flavored ChapStick kisses and surfing obsession. She listens in silence to each of my complaints about her world. And then I start to feel bad because I'm ragging on practically every detail of her life.

"No offense," I say, quickly. "I'm trying to say I'm sorry. I wish I'd understood before."

Melody shakes her head. "No, it's good to hear you say it. I told you my life wasn't perfect."

"You tried to but I never listened. And worse than that, I've been awful. I'm so sorry, Melo."

She smiles and says, "It's okay, Katie. I must admit, being you isn't so great, either. Ryan and Reese are exhausting. And you never told me how much you had to babysit for them. And that you didn't get paid, like, ever."

"I was embarrassed," I say, shifting in my seat. "Because maybe there's something wrong with my mom and Jeff for asking me all the time. Or maybe there's something wrong with me for getting so upset about it."

"Every once in a while would be fine, but your mom asks you to babysit every day," Melody says.

"I know."

"And the twins get up so early."

"I know!"

"And they are so loud. Plus, they never let up with the fighting," says Melody.

I nod, staring out the window. We are winding our way through the canyon and heading toward the tunnel. "Yeah, everything you're saying is true, but I still miss my life."

"I miss my life, too," says Melody. She glances at me nervously. "Um, want to switch back?"

"Wait, what?" I'm so surprised, I'm not sure what to say. Am I ready to go back to my old life? Ready to move back into my small, messy house? Ready to take care of the twins again, and be my not-so-gorgeous self? The funny thing is, I think I am. "Do you think we'll even be able to switch back?" I wonder.

She shrugs. "It's worth a shot, right? I mean, why not try? It should work if we both want it to."

"Okay," I say, squirming in my seat. "Let's try."

Melody grabs my hand and squeezes. I'm feeling good about this. Hopeful. We are getting closer to the tunnel and this could be the moment.

"Are you ready?" she asks.

I nod and close my eyes and hold my breath and wish to be myself again with all of my might.

The tunnel feels cold and I shiver, get goose bumps, even. Then I feel that familiar tingling sensation. Things are shifting and changing. Time is speeding up. The bus propels us forward. *It's working it's working it's working.*

At least I hope it is.

I feel someone beside me and I hope it's Melody.

Moments later I feel the warmth of the sun. Once I'm absolutely positive that we're out of the tunnel I open my eyes and take a breath.

Up ahead I see the sun and the sky and Crescent Moon Bay in all its glory. The sand and the ocean—the magic of the beach is right in front of us.

But better than that, I see my best friend, Melody. She's sitting on the seat right next to me, eyes shining with excitement and a big smile on her face. For the first time in ages, actually, I truly see her.

Goodbye Summer

It's the last day of summer—again! And I feel like there's so much to do, so much to squeeze in. Katie and I brought our bikes to the beach and we're racing down the path. The wind is whipping through my hair and we ride so fast we see a million beach scenes but all speeded up. Kids with red buckets, tanned ladies in floppy hats, old dudes with round hairy bellies, Rollerbladers in spandex, joggers in tank tops, skaters, surfers, and dogs. I even see a giant lizard on a leash. Frisbees fly through the air and footballs do, too. I love it: the salty air and the summer sun, the sparkling sea and the magic. Well, not the magic. I'm done with the magic for now. Regular life is complicated enough.

After a while Katie veers off the path and hops off her

bike. I follow her and we lock our bikes up at the nearest rack, kick off our shoes, and run toward the surf.

When we're ankle-deep we stop and gaze out. The sun is starting to set and the sky glows orange-pink.

"I can't believe we start seventh grade tomorrow," says Katie.

I don't say anything because I can believe it. I'm scared and excited, but most of all, I'm ready. I take a deep breath. "This is so gorgeous, I want to paint it," I say. "Capture it all on a giant canvas and hang it on my wall."

"Except your mom would never let you," Katie reminds me.

I shake my head. "Nope, she has no choice. I told her I'm redecorating. The rest of the house is hers but my room is my own."

Katie raises her eyebrows and looks at me, totally shocked. "And Debbie actually agreed to that?"

"She had to," I say, with a huge grin. "I told her I was sick of shopping, that I needed a real hobby. And that exercise is fine once in a while, but I'm not going to do her crazy workouts with her. Especially on Saturday mornings, because I signed myself up for this awesome art class downtown."

"That's so not mellow," Katie says, impressed.

I shrug. "Yeah, turns out there's such a thing as too mellow and that's not me anymore."

"That's awesome. When do you start?" Katie asks.

"Next week. I can't wait! Hey, do you want to sign up, too? Or do you have to babysit?"

Katie shakes her head. "No, thanks. Art isn't really my thing. But then again, neither is free babysitting. My mom and Jeff promised me they'd find a real babysitter for the twins. And when I do end up babysitting, they're actually going to pay me."

"That's amazing," I say. "Tell them to give me a call. I'd be happy to hang with the boys anytime."

"Anytime?" asks Katie, eyebrows raised.

"Well, maybe not anytime, but definitely sometime. I actually miss them."

"Hey, race you back to the bikes?" Katie asks.

Before I have a chance to answer she's sprinting up the beach, already halfway there.

An hour later we're boarding the bus again. It's the last shuttle of the day, our last ride of the summer.

"I cannot believe it's over," Katie says, leaning back as she pulls her hair up into a ponytail.

"Well, at least this time we got two summers for the price of one," I remind her.

"Thanks to the tunnel," Katie whispers as the bus pulls away from the curb. "I wonder if it'll work again. Maybe we should make another wish."

"You're crazy," I say, shaking my head. "Don't get any

ideas. I do not want to repeat this summer a third time and I do not want to trade places again."

"Neither do I," Katie says. "But I'm thinking . . . What if we wish for something else?"

"What do you mean?" I ask.

"Well, we know the tunnel is magic, but how magic is it? Like, can we wish for anything? The perfect boyfriend?"

"You thought you had a perfect boyfriend in Kevin," I remind her.

"I know. I guess I should've learned my lesson. He's a sweet guy, but we're definitely better off as friends. And not even good friends. Just regular I'll-high-five-you-in-the-hallway-and-maybe-sit-with-you-at-lunch-on-occasion type of friends. So, really I did you a favor by breaking up with him," Katie says.

I let out a laugh. "Um, I wouldn't go that far. It's probably something I should've done myself, especially since we're neighbors."

Katie cringes and shifts around in her seat. "Right. I guess that could get awkward. I'm sorry. Is he still avoiding you?"

I shake my head. "No, don't worry about it. We hung out last night. You know, just as friends. Kevin is still freaked out by my major personality change this summer, but it all worked out in the end. I think he's just relieved I'm back to acting like myself, no offense."

"None taken," says Katie. "But you're right. Maybe we should both wish for an amazing seventh-grade year."

I think about this for a moment. "But that can mean so many things . . ."

She smiles at me, mischievously. "Exactly!"

I bite my bottom lip. "I don't know. It makes me nervous, not being specific. I think we should play it safe and ride through the tunnel with our eyes wide-open."

"That's such a waste!" Katie says.

I giggle. "It's really not. Think about our last wishes, how hard the summer was. And there's no more beach bus after today. That means whatever you wish for you're stuck with until next summer."

"Unless the magic is in the tunnel and not the bus," Katie says.

"It could be both—I guess we'll never know. So isn't it better to be careful and avoid the potential for another disaster?"

Katie thinks about this for a minute. "Was the summer really a disaster? Maybe our wishes worked out perfectly. I mean here we are, best friends again."

"Exactly," I say, nodding. "We got what we wanted, so we should be happy. Quit while we're ahead."

Katie stares at the road in front of us. "I don't know. There's always room for improvement."

The tunnel is right in front of us and I'm afraid Katie's going to do something crazy.

"Let's just try to have a normal year," I say.

Katie smiles and says okay, but I can tell she doesn't mean it. She's made her decision. There's no point in arguing—she's too stubborn. We're in the tunnel and she's squeezing her eyes shut tight and holding her breath.

I feel a nervous tremor in the bottom of my belly. We're in the dark and I can sense that the universe is about to shift yet again. I should probably close my eyes and hold my breath, too, and wish to cancel out Katie's wish, but I don't think of that until it's too late.

"What did you wish for?" I ask once we're out of the tunnel. "Did it come true?"

"I think so," Katie says. "But it's way too soon to tell."

"Aren't you going to tell me what it is?" I ask.

Katie shakes her head, grinning like mad. "There's no fun in that!"

Now I'm getting scared. "Katie, what did you do?"

She won't tell me specifics, though.

Not even after I beg and plead.

She won't even give me a hint.

All she says is, "You'll see!"

ACKNOWLEDGMENTS

Special thanks to Janine O'Malley, Laura Langlie, Rachel Cohn, Morgan Matson, Coe Booth, Jenny Han, and Daniel Ehrenhaft.